DUMB DEATH

The sight of the Colt .45 in Skye Fargo's hand made the trail rat drop the gun he was holding on prim, proper, and all-too-tempting Priscilla Dale. Fargo stepped forward and kicked the weapon aside.

"Get out of here," Fargo said, "before I change my mind."

The man walked slowly toward his horse. Fargo led Priscilla by the arm to where his Ovaro waited when he heard the rustle of a shirtsleeve against leather. "Down," he yelled as he flung her face forward while two shots grazed his head.

Fargo rolled, firing three shots that blended together as the man slumped to the gound. The gun in his hand, a pocket pistol he'd pulled from inside his belt, fell from his fingers as he lay still.

"My God," Priscilla gasped.

Fargo shrugged. "Stupid men do stupid things," he said.

What he didn't say was that taking the job of watching over the greenest tenderfeet who ever tried to survive in the West might have been the stupidest thing the Trailsman had ever done . . . .

**Be sure to read the other books
in the exciting Trailsman series
about the Old West!**

THE
TRAILSMAN
162

REVENGE
AT
LOST CREEK

by

Jon Sharpe

A SIGNET BOOK

SIGNET
Published by the Penguin Group
Penguin Books USA Inc., 375 Hudson Street,
New York, New York 10014, U.S.A.
Penguin Books Ltd, 27 Wrights Lane,
London W8 5TZ, England
Penguin Books Australia Ltd, Ringwood,
Victoria, Australia
Penguin Books Canada Ltd, 10 Alcorn Avenue,
Toronto, Ontario, Canada M4V 3B2
Penguin Books (N.Z.) Ltd, 182–190 Wairau Road,
Auckland 10, New Zealand

Penguin Books Ltd, Registered Offices:
Harmondsworth, Middlesex, England

First published by Signet, an imprint of Dutton Signet,
a division of Penguin Books USA Inc.

First Printing, June, 1995
10 9 8 7 6 5 4 3 2

Copyright © Jon Sharpe, 1995
All rights reserved

The first chapter of this book previously appeared in *Rogue River Feud*,
the one hundred sixty-first volume in this series.

The Trailsman

Beginnings . . . they bend the tree and they mark the man. Skye Fargo was born when he was eighteen. Terror was his midwife, vengeance his first cry. Killing spawned Skye Fargo, ruthless, cold-blooded murder. Out of the acrid smoke of gunpowder still hanging in the air, he rose, cried out a promise never forgotten.

The Trailsman they began to call him all across the West: searcher, scout, hunter, the man who could see where others only looked, his skills for hire but not his soul, the man who lived each day to the fullest, yet trailed each tomorrow. Skye Fargo, the Trailsman, the seeker who could take the wildness of a land and the wanting of a woman and make them his own.

*1860, the Montana Territory
a land guarding the secrets of men
and the riddle of greed . . .*

1

It was one of those times when the big man with the lake blue eyes wished his hearing was not so acute. He was distinctly uneasy about his arrival in this flea-bitten little town. Skye Fargo didn't need complications, and he took another bite of the beef and bean sandwich on his plate as he sat in a corner of the saloon. The sandwich was good, the bourbon smooth, only the voices of the men on the other side of the thick wooden beam kept intruding.

"All we gotta do is screw her," the one said, a raspy voice. "Over and over. Hell, we can sure do that."

"I'm all for it. We can cut to see who does her first," another one said with a high-pitched guffaw.

"I'll bet she's a virgin. She's the kind, prim and prissy and all uptight. She won't recover for a year," a third voice said. "Never screwed a virgin before. I'll enjoy this."

"She's got the right name, too . . . Priscilla. I knew a Priscilla, once. She was an uptight little bitch, too," a fourth man put in, a low, growly voice. "When do we do her?"

"What's the matter with tonight . . . later?" the raspy voice answered. "It'll be easy. It's not like she'll be at home with her pa guardin' her."

"Maybe we oughtta think about it some more," the man with the high voice responded. Fargo finished the last of his sandwich and downed the bourbon.

"Why? We just take her and do it," the raspy voice said.

"That's right," the one with the low growl chimed in. "I need to get laid, and a little uptight virgin will be extra perfect."

"Besides, it always helps to combine business with pleasure," the answer came and with it the high-pitched guffaw.

Fargo felt himself frowning at the remark, unclear how it fit. The waitress came over, took his money, and he rose and walked from the saloon, slowing to cast a quick glance at the four men around the table. They were huddled together, still laughing, thoroughly ordinary in appearance, though one sported a high-crowned, black Stetson. Fargo walked on and stepped outside into the night air, then walked to where the Ovaro was tied to the hitching post. He pushed away the conversation he'd overheard. He wasn't keeper of the town's morals. And he wasn't even certain the men hadn't just been bragging—hollow boasting based on wishful thinking. He'd seen that often enough, he reminded himself as he swung onto the saddle and sent the magnificent horse with the jet black fore- and hindquarters and pure white section into the night.

He didn't need any more uncertainties, not on this strange undertaking. He had a tomorrow filled with them, and that was more than enough. Besides, all he had was a first name, Priscilla, and how was he going to track down a girl from just a first name? Damn, he swore. The damn conversation insisted on sticking in him, and he made a face as he pulled to a halt. He swore again. Someone had once told him that a conscience was the worst burden to put on a man. They were right. He grimaced as he turned the Ovaro around. He had to give it a try, if only for his own peace of mind. But it could be the proverbial needle in a haystack, he realized, and decided he had only one thing to go on: where *not* to look.

If this girl was as they had described her, he could cross out the dance hall and the local bordello. But that left God knows how many houses and farms in and around town. But his brow creased as something one of the men said worked its way through his mind. *It'll be easy. It's not like she'll be at home with her pa guardin' her.* That said she probably wasn't a part of one of the families in the area, and he spurred the Ovaro back to town. The town was a scroungy place, but it had a bank, a church, and a clapboard house that put itself forward as an inn. He had glimpsed all three when he'd ridden into town but a few hours earlier, and he drew up before the building with the small sign that proclaimed: CYPRESS INN.

He dismounted and walked into a dimly lit foyer, a public room with tables and chairs to one side and across from it, a desk and a counter where the desk register lay closed. A sallow-faced kid rose from behind the desk, stepped to the counter, and surveyed him with bored indifference. "Need a room?" he asked.

"No. Need some information. You have a young woman named Priscilla staying here?" Fargo answered.

"We don't go by first names," the youth said curtly.

"I suppose not, but I'd guess you don't have too

many young women staying here. A look at the register might tell me what I want to know," Fargo said.

"We don't give out our guests' names," the youth snapped. Fargo's glance went across the entranceway and took in the peeling paint, frayed curtains, and a stuffed chair with torn upholstery.

"I'm sure this is a very high-class operation, but I'm asking you to make an exception. It's for the young lady's good," Fargo said.

"Can't do it," the youth said, a crafty insolence coming into his eyes.

"Would a little offering persuade you to change your mind, say a gold dollar?" Fargo asked mildly.

"It might," the youth said.

Fargo's smile was pure affableness. The youth's mouth dropped open as a big hand was suddenly around his throat, the revolver pressed against his temple. "Then this ought to persuade you, too," Fargo said. "Open the goddamn register." The youth, now ashen-faced, opened the gray-covered register book with one hand, and Fargo released his grip and pulled the Colt back. "That's much more cooperative," Fargo said and let his eyes go down the page of the register. There weren't that many names, and his finger came to rest at one. "I'll be damned," he murmured. "Priscilla Dale." His lifted his eyes to the youth.

"Room four . . . end of hallway," the youth said.

"How long has she been here?" Fargo asked.

"Two days," he was told.

"Thanks for your help," Fargo said, holstering the Colt. The youth closed the register without looking up, and Fargo walked down a long hallway to the dim end where he found the door and knocked. He had to wait only a few moments before the door was opened, and he saw the young woman, a blue-gray robe tightly wrapped around her. She was tall, slender, the robe concealing most of her figure. "Priscilla Dale?" he asked.

"Yes," she said.

He took in a very young face, pretty in a fresh, scrubbed away. Ash blond hair had been pulled up atop her head—for bed, he supposed—and he saw eyebrows to match her hair. She was smooth-skinned and pale, with very round, very wide eyes that helped give her a little-girl appearance, a small nose, and a small mouth held more primly than lips ought to be held. Yet her light blue eyes held a cool, contained appraisal that was very adult.

"The name's Fargo . . . Skye Fargo. I heard some men talking about you in the saloon," he said.

Her wide eyes grew wider. "Talking about me?"

"Unless there's another Priscilla Dale in town," Fargo said.

"I doubt that," the young woman said.

"Me, too," Fargo agreed.

"Who were these men?" Priscilla Dale asked.

"Town loafers, I'd guess. I didn't get names."

"What were they saying?"

Fargo felt the moment of uncomfortableness poke at him as he sought a less crude way of putting it than the four men had used. "They said they were going to take you," he offered.

"Take me?" She frowned.

"Enjoy you. Pleasure themselves with you. You want me to be plainer, honey?" Fargo said.

"No, that won't be necessary. I think I quite understand," Priscilla Dale said. "But I think you must have misunderstood whatever you heard."

"There was nothing to misunderstand," Fargo grunted.

"You must have. It's just ridiculous. I don't even know anyone in town. Why should they pick on me?" she asked.

"Guess you took their fancy," Fargo said.

The very round, light blue eyes stayed cool as she studied his chiseled handsomeness. "And what do you suggest?" she asked.

"I could take you out of here, or stay here with you," Fargo said.

"Absolutely not," Priscilla Dale snapped. "I don't mean to sound ungracious, but I'm not going off with a total stranger or have one stay in my room. That's out of the question."

"You think I've come here to make my own move on you?" Fargo questioned.

"Frankly, I don't know what to think," she said coolly. "Let's say whatever you heard you heard wrong. I think that would be the most charitable explanation I can give."

Fargo felt irritation stab at him. She was a snippy, suspicious little thing, her wide-eyed little-girl appearance cloaking a very unyielding stiffness. Prim, he grunted silently. The lowlifes at the saloon had been right about that. "I've said my piece, honey. You take it from here," he told her.

"Thank you for coming," she said, very proper dismissal in her tone as she closed the door.

"Sure thing," Fargo snapped as he strode down the hallway and out to where the Ovaro waited. He swung onto the saddle and sent the Ovaro from the town at a fast canter, finally turned from the road, and went up a low slope to a stand of box elder. He refused to wonder why he was so annoyed. He'd told her—warned her. He'd done his duty by her. His conscience was clear, now. Hell what more could anyone ask?

He found a spot to halt and dismounted, pulled down his bedroll, undressed, and lay back. But he found sleep an uncooperative companion as he tossed and turned and pressed his eyes shut. He had no idea how long he wrestled with the night when he finally sat up, pulling his eyes open. "Ah, shit," he swore. "Goddamn stubborn, suspicious little package." It was only logic and reason pushing at him, he told himself, but he knew it was more. Conscience refused to be dismissed. It clung, like a wet leaf on a rock. Maybe it had been too much to expect her to take his offer, or believe his story about the men at the saloon. After all, as she'd said, he was a total stranger to her.

Maybe he'd been too quick to walk away from her. "Damn," he swore as he yanked on clothes and climbed onto the pinto. He set off at a gallop as he retraced steps back to the town. Slowing when he reached the inn, he reined to a halt in the still darkness and peered through the front entrance. He saw the youth asleep, head on his arms folded atop the desk, and he dismounted and entered the hotel with silent steps. Reaching the end of the hallway, he knocked on the door. There was no answer so he knocked again, then again, harder. There was still no answer, and he tried the door. It was locked, and his mouth was a tight line as he ran down the hall and outside where he raced around to the back of the inn. He saw the open window at once and knew its grim meaning. They had been there, and his eyes flicked to the ground.

The moon was nearly full, the hoofprints clear in the earth. He took a moment to kneel down and run his fingers over the prints. They hadn't more than a few minutes start, the indented places still very warm and moist. He was on the Ovaro seconds later, following the trail of hoofprints. The four men had ridden across a field, the prints easy to follow, and he saw them go over a small dip and into a line of woods, mostly hackberry. He slowed as he spotted the light, first, then the small house set back in the woods. He heard the sound of the men first, their voices loud, some slurred by liquor, and he dropped to the ground and moved to the house. They had left the door open, and Fargo moved to where he could partly see into the single room.

One of the men came into view, thin, with a loose shirt and torn Levi's, then the one with the high-crowned black hat. He found Priscilla Dale next, seated in a straight-backed chair, her knees held tightly together. They had pulled the robe from her, but she had on bloomers that fitted tight around her legs and a camisolelike top that left her arms and shoulders bare. He saw fear in her eyes, but also a cold contempt. The one with the black hat walked to her, and Fargo heard the other two men, but they were out of his line of vision. With a quick motion the man seized her and pulled her arms over her head. "Take off her bloomers, Jake," he said. "It's time we got some of this brand-new pussy."

"Scum. Rotten scum," Priscilla Dale spit out as she kicked at the second man, who grabbed for her legs, and Fargo heard the other two, still unseen, guffaw. The torn Levi's caught hold of her one leg, twisted, and Priscilla Dale cried out in pain. Fargo swore under his breath. He didn't want a bloodbath, especially when it might be Priscilla's. The black-hatted one would immediately use the young woman as a shield once he fired, Fargo realized, and the others would dive for the corners of the room out of his line of fire. That would still leave Priscilla trapped inside the house, still their hostage, and they'd know he was outside. He grimaced as he knew he had to make his first shot count for more than that.

He had to let it give Priscilla a chance to get out and cut down the odds some. His glance went to the kerosene lamp on the floor. He could shoot it out, he calculated, but would Priscilla think fast enough to get out or would she freeze in fright? He had to take the chance, he decided. He hadn't that many options open to him. Raising the Colt, Fargo took aim and fired, and the black-hatted man shouted in pain as he fell backward, one hand clasping his shoulder. Fargo had already shifted the Colt and fired again, and the room was plunged into darkness as the lamp shattered. "Run for it," Fargo shouted over the surprised curses that arose, and he dropped low as a shot whistled through the doorway.

He glimpsed Priscilla half crawling, half flinging herself forward, white bloomers a flash in the darkness. She was at the doorway, and he started to reach for her when three more shots came through the doorway and one grazed his head. He dropped flat and saw the young woman being pulled back into the house, trying to kick herself free but failing. Fargo rolled and came up on one knee against the edge of the doorjamb, cursing softly. It had failed. The girl was still their hostage. He heard muttered exchanges from inside the house, a sharp cry of pain from Priscilla as she was pushed into a corner. "Let the girl go. That's all I want," he called.

A moment of muttering followed. "Let her go?" a voice called back. "We'll put a bullet through her."

"Do that and you're dead men. Guaranteed," Fargo said.

"You going to rush us, you dumb bastard?" the voice said with a sneer.

"Nope. I'm going to wait for morning," Fargo answered.

Fargo heard the surge of muffled voices as they realized the advantage would swing with the dawn when he'd be able to pick them off as they tried to get out. He drew back from the edge of the doorway, reloaded the Colt, and rested on one knee. A voice came from inside the house. "Who the hell are you, mister?" it asked.

"Somebody who wants the girl," Fargo called back.

"She your woman?" the growly voice asked.

"She's not yours. That's all that matters," Fargo said.

"Let's talk about this. Step out where we can see you," another voice said.

"You boys have a real sense of humor," Fargo returned.

"You won't think it funny when you're dead," the man said.

"I'd guess it'll be dawn in about two hours," Fargo said, his voice casual as he rose to his feet. They were small-time. They hadn't the discipline to see it through. They'd try to make their way out. He had to be ready when they did, so he moved from alongside the doorway to the corner of the house where he went to the rear. There was but one side window, too small to crawl through. Their only way out was through the front door, and he allowed himself a moment of grim

18

satisfaction as he moved into the edge of the trees behind the front of the house.

Settling down on one knee, he prepared to wait, but found he had only some half hour of waiting when the growly voice called out. "Bert's bleeding bad from where you got him," the man said. "We've got to get a doc for him." Fargo didn't answer. "You hear me?" the man shouted. Fargo remained silent and listened to the muffled voices from inside the house. In moments the voice called out again. "You gonna answer us?" it asked. Fargo remained silent and heard more hasty exchanges. Finally, the growly-voiced man spoke up again. "We're coming out to get a doc, and we're taking her with us. You make one wrong move and she's dead, you hear me?"

Once more Fargo remained absolutely silent. They were dripping perspiration by now, he knew, their trigger fingers slippery. He stayed unmoving, hardly drawing a breath, his eyes on the doorway. The figures began to edge out, three of them, surrounding and holding Priscilla between them. They had left Bert behind, ostensibly to wait for them to fetch the doc. But he was probably waiting, watching from inside for Fargo to show himself. They were neither smart nor courageous, but they had a rodentlike caginess. He couldn't afford to take any chances, and he flattened himself on the ground, stretched out his arm, and took aim.

The one with the black hat had the gun against Priscilla's throat, the other two huddled beside her. Fargo let them turn for a moment and saw them sweep the trees in front of the house with long, nervous glances as they edged toward the horses at the far corner of the cleared space. He knew he could give them no more room. They'd shoot Priscilla out of fear or nervousness or just plain small-time meanness. His finger tightened on the trigger, and the shot exploded in the night. The high-crowned black hat flew from the man's head as he pitched forward. Fargo heard Priscilla's scream as the other two turned. One crumpled to the ground as Fargo's next shot exploded. The third one had gone into a crouch, and he was firing wildly into the trees until Fargo's shot cut him down.

Priscilla Dale had flung herself to the ground, and Fargo stayed motionless, his eyes on the house. "It's over. Come out," he called and waited. The figure appeared after a long moment, edging from the door, one shoulder bandaged, but a gun still in his hand. "Bad idea that didn't work," Fargo said as he rose to his feet. "Drop the gun." The man let the gun slide from his hand, and Fargo stepped forward and kicked the weapon aside. "Get out of here," he said. "Before I change my mind." The man started toward the horses, walking slowly, and Fargo took Priscilla Dale by the arm. He was steering her to where the Ovaro waited when he heard the sound, the rustle of a shirt-sleeve against leather. "Down," he yelled as he flung himself forward with her following, and two shots grazed his head.

He rolled, heard a third shot thud into the ground, and then he was firing, three shots that blended together almost as one, and the man slumped to the ground. The gun in his hand, a pocket pistol he'd pulled from inside his belt, fell from his fingers as he lay still. "My God," he heard Priscilla gasp, and she came to him again as he pushed to his feet, fingers digging into his arm.

"Stupid men do stupid things," Fargo said as he started to walk to the Ovaro, but she turned from him.

"I want to get my robe," she said and hurried into the house to reappear in moments, the blue-gray robe pulled tightly around her. He helped her into the saddle in front of him and rode slowly back to town and felt the slenderness of her inside his arms as he held the reins. But her rear, pressed back into his crotch, had a very soft roundness to it. "There's no way I can thank you," she said as they rode. "I was very wrong, not to listen to you."

"Can't blame you all that much," he said.

"I still don't understand any of it. I didn't know those men. I certainly didn't encourage them. I've only been here two days," she said.

"What brought you to Cypress?" Fargo asked.

"I came to meet some people. I arrived a few days early. But, as you said, they just took a fancy to me," Priscilla mused aloud.

"Probably," Fargo said, and she turned in the saddle to look at him with her round, wide eyes.

"What does that mean?" she asked.

"They said some things that stick inside me," he answered.

"Such as?"

"For one thing, they knew you were at the inn," he said.

"I don't suppose it'd be hard to have learned that," Priscilla Dale said. "They probably know all the town girls."

"True enough," Fargo agreed. "But then they said something about combining business with pleasure."

The light blue eyes stayed on him, a furrow creasing her smooth forehead. "I certainly can't imagine what that meant," she said.

"It could've meant somebody paid them to take you," Fargo ventured, and her frown deepened.

"Nonsense. I don't have any enemies," Priscilla Dale said.

"Sometimes we have enemies we don't know about," Fargo remarked as he rode to a halt in front of the inn. She was still frowning, rejecting his answer by the frown, as he helped her from the Ovaro, his hands almost encircling the very small waist.

"Again, I've no way to thank you," Priscilla Dale said, standing before him. "It was a wonderful thing to do, and I'll be forever grateful to you for it." She pushed her hand out, shook his with a firm grip, and he smiled inwardly. The one word flew into his mind. *Proper.* She was being properly grateful. Not warmly, not spontaneously, not affectionately, but properly. Priscilla Dale was all properness. He doubted she'd ever done anything that was not proper. Proper and prim, he had to admit, and her voice cut into his thoughts. "Perhaps we'll meet again sometime, and I'll be able to do something wonderful for you," she said. "Though I can't imagine what it might be," she added thoughtfully.

"You never know," Fargo said.

"Thank you again," she said, withdrawing her hand, and he half expected her to curtsy. But she turned and walked quickly into the inn. Fargo sent the Ovaro on at a walk and let himself feel good. Hell, good deeds were supposed to make you feel good, he murmured. God knows what he'd be feeling come tomorrow, he reminded himself.

2

Fargo lay in the morning sun, the circumstances that had brought him here parading through his mind. He welcomed the review. Each step had been tinged with strangeness, the last one the strangest of all. He kept his eyes closed, and it all unfolded itself again with crystal clarity. Jim Henricks had gotten him into it. He'd just finished breaking a new trail for Jim through the North Dakota Snake Creek country, one of many he'd done for Jim Henricks. He was in the cattleman's office when Jim leaned forward across his desk.

"Got a job for you, Fargo, but not for me," Jim Henricks had said. "Real good money for you and you'll be doing a favor for an old friend of mine, Tom Sprague."

"I'm listening, especially about the money part," Fargo said.

Jim Henricks reached into a desk drawer and pulled out a bundle of dollar bills, enough to make anyone's eyes widen. "Tom Sprague asked me to deliver it to you," Henricks said. "It's payment in advance."

"For what? That's a powerful lot of money," Fargo said.

"He wants you to take a group of people on a search for a stash of gold. If they find it, it's theirs."

"Why'd he pick me?" Fargo queried.

"Two reasons. He heard about the Trailsman, heard you were the very best, and he wanted someone with the integrity to keep his agreement no matter what. He told me he heard you fit the bill and I agreed," the cattleman said.

"He told you all this personally?"

"By mail, though Tom Sprague and I go back a long way. He's been in the Montana Territory for some years now," Henricks said. "At Rockville near the Dakota border."

Fargo counted the bundle of bills and emitted a low whistle. It was the kind of money one didn't turn down. "How does your friend Tom know about this stash of gold?" Fargo asked.

"He put it there." Henricks said and laughed as Fargo's eyebrows shot upward. "Let me tell you about Tom Sprague," he said. "He's a fascinating man. Some would say a strange man. He's very well educated, very smart. We were real close years ago, but our relationship has been by mail the last few years. For years he roamed everywhere, prospecting for gold."

"Seems he finally hit it," Fargo said.

"Yes, though most men would've spent it, but Tom stashed it away. He took only enough to come back East, want to school again, and became a teacher, a professor at some college."

"All the time he kept the gold stashed away?"

"That's right. He told me he wanted it safe for his old age. Professors don't retire with much, he said."

"Then why is he giving these people a chance to find it?" Fargo questioned.

"Now, that's one I can't answer. It beats me, but

that's what he wants. He sent me the money to hire you and wrote that if you agreed to take the job, he'd be sending you a letter. He even had me hire a standby courier to bring your answer to him," Henricks said.

Fargo eyed the stack of bills again. It was just too good an offer to turn down. "Tell him he's got himself the Trailsman," Fargo said after another moment's thought.

"Good. I'll send that courier off right away. He'll be sending his letter to you by return courier so you can wait around a few days as my guest at the ranch. Good beef and good bourbon. That ought to satisfy you," Henricks said.

"Definitely." Fargo laughed, and that had been the start of it. Henricks had been right about Tom Sprague's letter. It came by courier less than a week later, and Fargo read it with the cattleman at his elbow.

Dear Fargo,

I'm real pleased our agreement is sealed. You've been paid in full. That was my part of the agreement. Trying to find the gold for the others will be yours. That's why I chose you, because you are a man who will stick to his agreement.

All those you'll be taking are family, some close, some distant. They've all been told about the gold. That's what is bringing their greedy little souls to the prize. I also told them about hiring you. Your talents will be my gift to them.

They will be meeting on the fifteenth day of next month, a half mile north of a town called Cypress in the Montana Territory. You will meet them there. The gold lies northwest. That is all you need to know for now. But before meeting the others, you will go to the bank in town. My final instructions will be waiting there for you.

Tom Sprague

Fargo lowered the letter and cast a glance at Jim Henricks. "Strange, very strange, but then you said he was a strange man," Fargo commented.

"But a fascinating one. I've been sorry we haven't been able to see each other over the recent years. I always enjoyed Tom Sprague's mind and his storehouse of knowledge. But many people found him a difficult man to get along with," Henricks said.

"There's not a word in here on why he's doing this." Fargo mentioned.

"That's true, but you may find that out in his final instructions. I think you're going to enjoy this trip," the cattleman said.

"Why do I keep feeling just the opposite?" Fargo returned.

"Because you've a skeptical and suspicious nature, my friend." Henricks laughed, and that had been the beginning of it.

When he made his way to Cypress and the bank, events grew even stranger and his apprehensions deeper. The bank president had a large envelope waiting for him, but nothing much else to say. It appeared Tom Sprague had treated him with the same efficient but compartmented procedure with which he treated everyone. Fargo took the envelope to a hawthorn at the edge of town and sat down to look inside. He found that the large envelope held a number of smaller pieces of paper, each bearing a number and a half dozen lines of neat handwriting. A letter accompanied the contents of the envelope in the same neat handwriting, and he read it aloud to himself.

Mr. Fargo,
   By the time you read this I will be dead.

Fargo halted and reread the first line again. "God-damn," he muttered and went on.

Enclosed is the death certificate from the doctor and the burial deed from the undertaker in Rockville. Of course, I expected this. The doctors told me it was but a matter of weeks before it would happen. Everything in our agreement remains the same. You will carry through in every respect.
   But now you can understand why I didn't go back for the gold. It was of no use to me anymore. However, if the less than sterling members of my family want the gold, and show up to find it, they'll have to work for it. I have enclosed a number of clues for you, without which I doubt even you could find it. Good luck to you all.
                                                    Tom Sprague
P.S. I should warn you, there may be others who will come after the gold. I was perhaps too loose-tongued one night when I'd had too much to drink.

Fargo had folded the letter, his lips pursed, took another glance at the other pieces of paper in the envelope, and decided they could wait. He had pushed everything into his saddlebag and decided he needed a good beef sandwich, a good bourbon, and then a good night's sleep before meeting with Tom Sprague's relatives. But Priscilla Dale had come next, an interruption in the strange agreement he'd gotten himself into. However now he'd go on, and he sat up and stretched in the morning sun. Somehow, it seemed all the more important to go on, not just a matter of personal integrity, but an agreement sealed by greater forces.
Fargo rose, found a small stream, and leisurely

washed and dressed. There'd be plenty of time for hurrying, he was certain. Finally, he rode from town, headed north, and saw the cluster of wagons alongside the road. He made a quick count and came up with seven, a hodgepodge collection of vehicles. It seemed most of the occupants had left their wagons and were collected on the ground, watching him approach. When he reached them and came to a halt, two young men stepped forward, one with a pouty, weak face, the other taller and wearing a belligerent, unfriendly attitude as plain as the checked shirt he had on.

"You must be Fargo," he said.

"Bull's-eye," Fargo answered and offered a smile. The man didn't return it. "First thing I want to do is get acquainted with everybody," Fargo said.

"First thing we want you to do is turn around and be on your way," the man said.

"We?" Fargo echoed and shot a glance at two men and two women standing behind him. Both looked away, but not before he caught the uncertainty in their faces. It was more than enough for Fargo. He brought his eyes back to the young man in front of him. "First off, who are you, sonny?" he asked.

"Don't call me sonny," the youth snapped.

"Give me a name," Fargo said, taking in the man's small, thin mustache, darting eyes, slicked-down black hair, and thin figure.

"Harlan Brody. This is my brother, Jerry," he said with a gesture to the other man. Jerry Brody's pouty face remained impassive under a receding hairline. But he had a powerful, chunky build that didn't fit the weakness in his face.

"And you're family," Fargo said.

"Tom Sprague's still married to our sister," Harlan Brody said.

"Not any longer. Tom Sprague died," Fargo said and heard the collective gasp from the others. "Now, why do you want me to be on my way?"

"We're going to go it by ourselves, no strangers," Harlan Brody said.

Fargo smiled tolerantly. "You won't find steer shit by yourselves," he said.

"I think maybe we ought to listen to the man," someone said from the wagons.

"Besides, I made an agreement with Tom Sprague. I'm going to carry it through," Fargo said.

Harlan Brody's sullen face darkened further. "You're going to listen to me, not them," he said.

"Go away, sonny," Fargo said. "Go sit down someplace."

Harlan Brody yanked the gun from his holster, a Smith & Wesson six-shot, single-action piece with a steel frame and a fluted cylinder, a good gun in the right hands. "I'm going to be nice to you, Fargo. I'm going to show you why you're going to listen to me," Harlan Brody said. Turning, he glanced around, and his eyes came to rest on a line of cardinal flowers, their long, three-foot stalks of green leaves topped with brilliant red flowers standing in a neat row. He took aim, fired, the first flower exploding, took aim on the second and shot its red leaves off, went carefully down the row until he'd shot the tops from six of the flowers. Holstering the gun, he turned to Fargo and looked pleased with himself. "I'd say I've made my point," he remarked.

Fargo stayed in his saddle, let a sigh escape, and then the Colt seemed to fly into his hand. He fired, six shots that sounded as though they were one long explosion, and the flowers erupted in a shower of red that became a scarlet cascade. When he finished, the six stalks had been severed in the time it had taken Harlan Brody to sever his first one. Fargo looked down at Brody as he calmly reloaded and enjoyed the awe on the youth's face. "Now, what was that about making points, sonny?" he remarked. Harlan Brody didn't reply, but he swallowed hard as he turned away, and Fargo slid from the Ovaro. "Now, let's all get better acquainted," he said and faced a man and a woman, the man stoop-shouldered, almost cowed, balding, middle-aged, the woman standing very straight, her head held high, a large-framed body with a commanding attitude.

"I'm Sarah Dowd. This is my husband, Jake," she said in a crisp voice, and Fargo knew who wore the pants in the Dowd family, figuratively if not actually. He let his eyes go over an old Conestoga, a very worn piece with splits in the sideboards and wheels that were tilted on worn axles. "We're cousins of Tom's," Sarah Dowd said.

"See if you can tighten your axles," Fargo said as he moved to the next wagon and faced another man and woman.

"Ed Forstmann," the man said. He had a pleasant face with unruly brown hair on a thick-set frame. "This is my wife, Myra," Ed Forstmann said.

"Hello," Myra said in a cheery voice. She was younger than Ed by some ten years, Fargo guessed, with a brassy pleasantness that made him suspect she'd once been a dance-hall girl. Blond hair touched up with peroxide and too much eye makeup added to the picture, but she was still fighting to retain a curvy figure. Their wagon was a cut-under Owensboro where they'd built a frame for a square canvas top over it.

"Cousins, too?" Fargo asked, and both nodded.

Fargo went to the next wagon, a two-horse farm wagon with extra heavy hubs and a set of high bows that held the arch of canvas above an overloaded interior where slats of a bed stuck out from the rear along with the legs of a chair. A woman regarded him with halfway amused, dark blue eyes, dark hair pulled back, a broad face that was still attractive in an unvarnished way. She was mid-thirty, perhaps pushing forty, Fargo guessed, but an earthy vibrancy to her reinforced by a deep-breasted frame that filled a white, scoop-necked blouse and a skirt that was tight around strong, full-thighed legs. "Donna Sprague," she said and smiled as Fargo's brows lifted.

"You expected an older woman," she said.

"I didn't expect a wife," Fargo answered. "But if I had, you'd be right."

"We married when I was very young. I tried. I could never please him and we separated. Now I figure I'm owed some of his damn gold," Donna Sprague said.

"That's honest enough. I'll try to get it for you," Fargo said, and Donna Sprague smiled, a wide, warm smile that brought out the earthy attractiveness in her broad face.

"Good. I like you, Fargo, but I already did when you put Harlan in his place just now. He's a fool. So's Jerry," she said.

"Not a very sisterly attitude," Fargo remarked.

"Because they're my brothers? Only because we had the same mother. I haven't seen either of them for years. But Jerry's always been under Harlan's thumb. Don't trust either of them," the woman said.

"I'll remember that," Fargo said as he walked on to halt before a couple and their daughter, whom he guessed to be about twelve years old.

"Abel and Betsy Thiemann," the man said. "This is our daughter, Minnie." Fargo nodded at the girl. She barely acknowledged him, a listless child, he took note, absolutely devoid of personality with not a pretty bone in her. Perhaps she was very aware of that, he wondered. They had a big cut-under Owensboro wagon and were using heavy tarpaulins to cover the contents.

"More cousins?" Fargo asked.

"Yep. We're sure hoping you can lead us to that gold," Abel Thiemann said with a booming voice.

"I'll be trying," Fargo said.

"You call on us if we can help in any way," Betsy Thiemann said, and she was as cheerful and open as her daughter was withdrawn. Fargo nodded and walked on to a heavy, unwieldy hay wagon that had been converted to a haulage rig with a canvas top. A man and a woman stood alongside it, the man with a heavy beard and a big belly that overflowed loose pants.

"Sam Grafton," the man said and stepped forward to shake hands. "My wife, Nedda," he added and gestured to the woman beside him. Sam Grafton breathed hard even with a few steps, Fargo took note. The woman wore a shapeless dress, but her breasts managed to push out attractively, and he took in a pleasantly pretty face and guessed she was ten years younger than Sam. "Nedda's a cousin on her mother's side," Sam Grafton explained.

"Certainly cousins aplenty here," Fargo said.

"Well, the Forstmanns, the Dowds, and us were always good friends. Guess we're the ones that kept the family together, such as it was. Tom never made much bother about the family," Sam Grafton said.

"Well, he has now," Fargo said and walked on to halt before the next wagon, then felt a wave of surprise roll over him. "I'll be damned," he said and frowned and saw the very round, very big eyes regard him with quiet, cool amusement.

"I watched you as you rode up. You're not the only one surprised," Priscilla Dale said.

"Where do you fit in here?" Fargo queried.

"I'm Tom Sprague's niece, though I admit it's been years since I've seen him," Priscilla said. Fargo's glance went to her wagon, and his mouth tightened as he took in a two-seat surrey with the rear seat removed and a tarpaulin top put on over the fringed top so that it made closed sides. She had one horse in the shafts and another pack horse tied on behind. The very round light blue eyes peered at him, and she was quick to pick up things, he found. "Something wrong with my wagon?" she questioned.

"Too light," Fargo grunted.

"I believe in traveling light," she said.

"I didn't see a wagon shop in town or I'd have you turn it in for something heavier," Fargo said.

"There isn't one and my surrey will do perfectly well," Priscilla said with a touch of loftiness.

"I hope you're right, honey," he said and stepped back to where he could address all of them at once. "Now that we've met, you can get yourselves ready to roll," he said. "I've agreed to do a job and I'm going to do it. Anyone who doesn't like the way I'm doing it can cut out. Otherwise, I won't be engaged in any debates. We won't be taking any votes on anything. Anybody doesn't like that can go your own way now. Any questions?"

No one spoke up, and Fargo nodded. He was being both harsh and honest. He'd long ago learned there was but one right way to lead, especially a collection of anxious greenhorns, and that was to lead. And hope you were right, he added to himself. Harlan and Jerry Brody had said no more than the others, but a quick glance at their sullen faces told him they'd be trouble. As the others readied their horses and wagon gear, Fargo returned to the Ovaro, reached into his saddlebag, and pulled out the piece of paper Tom Sprague had marked with a bold number 1. He sat quietly in the saddle as he read the neat handwriting.

Fargo—
   This is your first helpful clue. This, and those that will follow, are equally important. I suggest you do not disregard any. It will be virtually impossible to find the gold without going from each step to the next, I assure you.
   There is a river. On both sides it is bordered by the beauty of wild cherry trees. Cultures over the ages, from the ancient Greeks and the caliphs of Arabia to English soothsayers, have attached meanings to flowers and trees, innocence to the daisy, sincerity to the fern, boldness to the larch, prudence to the mountain ash, and so forth. Strangely, the wild cherry tree was considered to mean deception. Something to think about.

                                                                T.S.

Fargo put the piece of paper away, his lips pursed. He had the distinct feeling that the late Tom Sprague was toying with them all and that included himself. It

34

gave him a strange feeling, one he didn't much like. He glanced about, saw the others were ready and waiting, and he rode ahead and waved them on. Sprague's letter had said they'd be heading northwest, and he turned the Ovaro in that direction and set a leisurely pace.

The others followed in a ragged line, Donna Sprague first, then the Forstmanns in their cut-under Owensboro, then Harlan Brody driving his brother, and behind them rolling in a pair, the Dowds and the Thiemanns. The rest followed along, and he noticed that Priscilla Dale kept off to herself.

The land was mostly clean, some underbrush of shadscale and green sage and some rolling hills mostly planted with hackberry. It was easy for horses and wagons, and he had led the way into the afternoon when he spotted a horse and rider hurrying after them, and he called a halt. Riding a buff-color quarterhorse, the man came to a halt in front of him, and Fargo took in a gray formal jacket with velvet lapels, a matching top hat, and dark trousers. The cutaway jacket was the kind he'd seen on a hundred gamblers, and he noticed the slightly frayed cuffs and scuffed velvet of one lapel.

"Sorry I'm late," the man said with a smile. He had a sharp face, made of angles, with crinkles under his gray eyes and a jutting jaw. He tipped his hat, and Fargo saw smoothly combed black hair.

"You family, too?" Fargo questioned.

"Byron Sprague," the man said. "I'm Tom's nephew. You're the Trailsman he told us would lead the way."

"Bull's-eye," Fargo said and let his eyes move up

35

and down Byron Sprague. "I'd say you're a gambling man."

"Bull's-eye," Byron Sprague echoed with a laugh. "That's why I'm here. I'm a gambling man and I'm gambling this might just be a winning ticket."

Fargo glanced at the packroll behind the man's saddle. "You believe in traveling light, too," he said.

"Don't all gambling men?" Byron Sprague laughed and drew a smile and a nod of agreement from Fargo. He let his eyes go past Fargo to the others. "Hello, Abel, hello Betsy," he called out. "And hello, Sam. I wondered if you'd be here."

"We got a letter, just as you did, Byron," Sam Grafton said.

"Didn't realize any of you knew each other before today," Fargo put in.

"Some of us have known each other for years," the gambling man said, and Fargo saw the Thiemanns and the Graftons nod. He also caught a glint of amusement in Donna Sprague's eyes.

"You know everyone here?" he asked her.

"Only heard about them," she said. "But it seems Tom notified just about everybody who was family."

"Fall in line. We're moving on," Fargo said, spurred the Ovaro forward, and wondered, with a quick glance at Byron Sprague, if they were not all gamblers on this trip.

Another hour brought dusk, and Fargo found a place to camp alongside a stand of hackberry. Sam Grafton made a small fire, and the others gathered around it with their own food. Byron Sprague was garrulous and added a note of friendly humor that touched everyone but the Brody brothers. Priscilla, Fargo noted, sat a little apart from everyone else, and when the meal ended, he decided to give the Ovaro a quick brushing. He was using the sweat scraper and the curry from his equipment pouch when Priscilla passed beside him.

"I'm so glad you're the one leading us," she said. "After what you did for me last night, I know you're a man of moral strength, a person who believes in self-lessness over selfishness, principle over pleasure."

Her sincerity was mirrored in the very round eyes, and with it a touch of prim imperiousness, as though she were handing out approval as a grade. "Remind me to polish my halo," he said.

"Don't sell yourself short, Fargo," she said, her tone more reprimand than warmth. "Men like you are few and far between."

"Don't go looking for saints, honey. They're pretty damn few and far between, too," he said, not un-gently. Her lips pursed as she thought about his words.

"Good night, Fargo," she said and hurried to her tarpaulin-covered surrey, her round little rear moving nicely and firmly, a kind of prim beauty of its own. He smiled, then took his bedroll into the edge of the trees and saw Byron Sprague was using a bedroll set out near the Brody wagon. Donna Sprague stepped from her wagon for a moment, and under a light nightgown he could see the outlines of her large breasts and was surprised at how well-placed they were for their size, no sag in them at all. She returned to the wagon, but not before he glimpsed the curve of strong thighs. He let sleep come to him and was the first to wake, wash, and dress when morning came.

He had thought about the expedition and the tone of Tom Sprague's letters and clues, and when breakfast was finished, he spoke up. "There's something I think you all ought to know," he said. "This isn't going to be an easy ride. Tom Sprague has seen to that. He's giving you a chance at a lot of gold, but getting it won't be easy."

"He tell you that?" Sarah Dowd asked.

"In his way," Fargo said.

"We didn't expect he'd make it easy, not him," Abel Thiemann said, and Fargo heard the bitterness in his voice.

"Good, then you won't be fooling yourselves," Fargo said.

"I never fool myself, Fargo," Byron Sprague put in. "I'm a gambling man, remember. You win big or lose big. That's the only way to play."

"You getting cold feet?" Harlan Brody called out.

"You only wish." Fargo smiled. "Move out." He climbed onto the Ovaro and started northwest again. But this time he left the others behind and rode through a series of low hills, turned into higher ground, and his eyes swept the land ahead. He searched for the telltale blue ribbons that meant water, spied a half dozen but decided they were all too small to call a river. But he saw a gulley perfect for the wagons and returned to lead them through it. He had them rest the horses in midafternoon and watched Priscilla rest against her rig as the sun grew hot. She still kept her blouse buttoned to the neck, he saw, though her cheeks had a slight flush to them. When it was time to move on, he rode past her. "Unbutton some, Prissy. Modesty isn't worth heatstroke," he said.

"I won't be getting heatstroke, and don't call me Prissy. I hate that name," she said.

"Then unbutton. That's an order," Fargo said and

set the pinto into a trot. "Keep heading northwest," he called to the Thiemanns as he rode past. Once again, he rode ahead and climbed up onto a small ridge atop a low hill to scan the terrain below. A frown pressed across his brow as, almost at the horizon line, he saw the long blue stripe sparkling in the sunlight. It had substance, even at this distance, and he returned to the others and led them toward the spot. Dusk came too quickly, though, and he decided to camp and reach the place the following day. A thick stand of box elder provided a shield from the hot winds, and he let the wagons pull up wherever they wished.

Priscilla again drew up a little distance from the others, and he rode to her rig as she dismounted. She still had the blouse buttoned to the neck, but perspiration soaked much of the garment, and it clung to breasts that were suddenly revealingly shaped with long curves sloping to full, upturned bottoms where tiny points pressed into the damp material. "Maybe you didn't hear me give you an order," Fargo said evenly.

"I heard," Priscilla said, the round light blue eyes returning a glance of haughty calm. "I'll obey any order you give concerning your authority here, your job on the trail. That's within your province. I'm not obeying orders regarding my personal dress. Sorry, but I hope you'll understand."

He swung from the Ovaro and knew she didn't catch the tightness in his smile. "I've something for you to understand, honey. Any order I give you concerns the trail. There's no separating orders. Maybe you won't understand why I tell you what to do or how and when to do it, but you're going to do it."

The haughtiness stayed in the very round eyes. "I

don't see how the way I dress has anything to do with the trail or your authority," she insisted.

Fargo blew a sigh at her. "I'm still feeling patient with you so I'll explain. You lucked out today. You didn't keel over from the heat of wearing that blouse all buttoned up. You got yourself all sweated up so your blouse is sticking to your tits real nice and I like that. But you could've passed out instead, and then we'd lose time and have to take care of you and I wouldn't like that. So when I told you to loosen that blouse, it was about what was best for you and everybody else and that's part of being a trailsman. You'd best understand that and understand it real quick because I'm out of patience."

He smiled inwardly as he saw her quickly fold her arms over her breasts as she turned and climbed into the surrey. But he'd seen the flash of resentful acceptance in her eyes and that was enough.

He took his bedroll down and started for the edge of the box elders as dark fell when he heard Donna Sprague's voice. "Little touch of mutiny," she said, soft amusement in her tone, and he halted alongside her overloaded farm wagon. "Couldn't help overhearing," she said, smiling at him.

"Nothing I can't handle," Fargo said.

"I'm sure of that, big man," Donna Sprague said, and he saw the amusement dance in her gray eyes. "You could've been a lot less patient with her."

"She came close to a rough experience a few nights back. I happened to be around. Guess I'm still feeling a little sorry for her," Fargo said.

"I'm sure she appreciates it, in a proper way," Donna Sprague said and smiled.

"Bull's-eye." Fargo laughed and strode on. The

woman could read others, he took note, probably a combination of instinct and experience. He rolled out his bedroll, chewed on some cold beef strips, and waited till the others retired to their wagons before starting to shed clothes. He was down to only trousers when he saw the figure moving toward him with silent steps. Automatically, his hand closed around the Colt at his side, and then the modest moonlight let him see the light blue bathrobe wrapped tightly around the slender shape. He sat up, then she found him and changed directions. "Didn't expect company and certainly not you," Fargo said, relaxing his hand around the revolver.

"I'll only be a minute. I came to say I'm sorry about our little misunderstanding," Priscilla said, her voice firm.

"I didn't have any misunderstanding," Fargo said and saw her eyes flick over the muscled smoothness of his chest, look away, and flick back again.

"I suppose not," she said. "I should have known you had a proper reason for telling me to unbutton my blouse, especially after what you did for me the other night. I know you're an unusual man of unusual principles." Fargo nodded as he smiled inwardly. She wasn't apologizing. She was explaining. She held to her own principles, but she was having trouble not looking at his muscled torso. "Good night, Fargo," she said, suddenly abrupt, and he watched her hurry away, holding the robe tightly around her.

Perhaps Priscilla Dale was learning to unbend some, he mused as he lay back and drew sleep to himself until the new day came. When he finished dressing, he went to where the others gathered themselves, accepted a cup of coffee from Sarah Dowd, and saw

Harlan and Jerry Brody closeted together. They were planning something. They had been doing so for the past few days, keeping to themselves, whispering, a furtiveness about their movements they hadn't the brains to hide. He finished the coffee, swung into the saddle, and led the way forth to find Byron Sprague riding beside him, still wearing his gray frock coat.

"You have seen something, my friend," the man said.

"Yes. How'd you know?" Fargo asked with some surprise.

"A gambling man learns how to read the little things about the other players, how some men's eyes narrow when they get good cards, how others grow quiet when they sense a winning hand while some grow extra hearty and others lick their lips."

"And what did you read about me, gambling man?" Fargo smiled.

"You're sitting your horse differently. Your body is talking differently. You're onto something," Byron Sprague said, and Fargo laughed.

"Very good. You might just hold a winning hand in this gold stakes," Fargo said.

"You still feel it won't be an easy win?" the man asked.

"I'm sure it won't. I'm sure Tom Sprague planned it that way," Fargo said, and the other man nodded.

"You know my motto, Fargo. Play hard. Win big or lose big," Byron Sprague said and peeled his horse away as Fargo put the Ovaro into a fast trot. It was on the other side of a low hill, the others following a few thousand yards back, when he came in sight of the river. His eyes narrowed as saw the wide banks of wild cherry trees that bordered both sides of the river.

He rode through the trees to halt beside the river, then sat quietly until the wagons caught up with him. He was still staring at the river when they did, his jaw tightly set.

"What is it, Fargo?" Sarah Thiemann asked.

"This is your first breakthrough. This is the river Tom Sprague described for me," Fargo said.

"Why aren't you looking happy?" John Dowd asked.

"I'm bothered. He led you to this river to cross, but he gave another message. He wrote about how the ancients considered the wild cherry tree a symbol of deception. That means something, some sort of warning, I'd say," Fargo explained.

"Nonsense," Betsy Thiemann said. "That was just some of Tom's talk. He always liked to show off how much he knew."

"That's right," Sam Grafton agreed. "He always wanted to impress others."

Fargo's eyes continued to scan the river. Tom Sprague's words had not been included to show off. They were no exercise in idle erudition. He had planned every detail of this venture with great care, Fargo had come to conclude as he was starting to take the measure of the man. The words he had set down all meant something, Fargo was convinced. All he had to do was find out what.

ripples.

3

Fargo's lake blue eyes were narrowed as he slowly
scanned the river. He looked for those signs others
would fail to see, the flow of the water on the surface, the small variations that could indicate cross-
currents, tiny swirls that might mean a riptide, a
change of color that could mean a sudden drop in
depth. But he saw nothing to cause him any alarm,
the surface indicating a steady current moving
leisurely. He walked the horse close to the edge of
the shore and watched the water lap at the bank,
studying the movement of the ripples. Their length,
velocity, straightness, or sinuousity could tell him
what kind of river bottom he might find. But again,
there was nothing to alarm him.

He turned back to where the others waited and grimaced inwardly. There was something wrong. The
feeling persisted inside him. Tom Sprague, with an almost pixieish kind of smugness, had given a warning.
But Fargo realized he hadn't been able to discover its
meaning. He was left with crossing the river, which
had quickly become a kind of riddle. The others
waited with tense impatience, he saw, and he scanned
the wild cherry trees. They ran for at least a mile on
each side and were an impossibility to check out indi-

vidually. Besides, Tom Sprague had written that they were a symbol of deception, not the deception itself.

Swearing inwardly, he halted before the others. "I'm going to cross first," he said, and they watched as he moved the pinto into the river. He felt the horse's hooves take hold in the soft soil of the river bottom. No excessive pulling told him there was no unusually soft mud, and he steered the Ovaro to midriver. He was nearing the center when the river grew deeper, and he felt the horse beginning to swim, still occasionally touching bottom. He grunted in satisfaction. The wagons would be able to cross without sinking over their tops, though their horses would have to swim. He had reached directly in the center of the river when he felt the sudden surge of water as it pulled on the horse. A bottom undercurrent, he took note, not uncommon and not strong enough to give the Ovaro a problem.

He continued on, feeling the pull of the undercurrent himself. It continued until he was well past the midway point in the river, and he continued on to the opposite bank. He let the horse rest for a few moments while he scanned the wild cherry trees and saw nothing but their oblong green leaves and white flowers. He recrossed the river and again felt the pull of the undercurrent in midriver, somewhat stronger this time. But the wagons were heavy enough to handle it, except possibly Priscilla's surrey, he murmured to himself. When he reached the shore, he went to where she waited atop the driver's seat and took a long look at the surrey.

"There's an undercurrent in midriver that seems to vary in pull. If you feel yourself being pushed sideways, don't fight it. That can get you turned over in a

45

light rig," he told her. "You go downriver with it, let it take your horse and your wagon as you edge your way to shore at an angle. Soon as you're past midriver, you'll make shore. Understand?" She nodded and Fargo motioned to the others. "You'll cross in pairs. Leave a dozen feet between yourselves. The Graftons and Donna Sprague, first. Brody and Jake Dowd next. The rest of you pair up, but I want Priscilla to draw up at the rear." He moved the Ovaro into the river and watched Sam Grafton send his converted hay wagon into the water, Donna Sprague entering a dozen feet downriver from him. She drew parallel to the Graftons, and they started across together. Fargo reined up to the side where he could see the others pairing up as they entered the river, Priscilla the last to enter with Byron Sprague riding alongside her.

Fargo moved forward, riding just ahead of the first pair of wagons, and he saw Donna Sprague's overloaded wagon had already sunk into the river above its extraheavy hubs. But it rolled steadily under the pull of the two-horse brace, and he glanced at Grafton. The man was taking in great gulps of air as he held the reins, and Fargo wondered about his ability to withstand a long and arduous trip. Nedda Grafton sat close beside him, one hand on his shoulder. The next two wagons were drawing closer to the first two, and Fargo called to them. "Keep your distance," he shouted and saw them quickly rein back. Donna and the Graftons were near midriver, and Fargo felt the pull on the Ovaro, stronger than before. It was plainly an uneven, fluctuating current, and he could feel the horse tightening its foreleg and hindquarter muscles.

He was moving the Ovaro forward through the undercurrent when he heard Nedda Grafton scream, and he half turned in the saddle to stare at the huge tree trunk of gnarled roots. It rose from the river as it came up under the Grafton's wagon as though it were some apparition with a hundred clawing arms, surfacing from the depths of hell. "Goddamn," Fargo swore as he saw the Grafton's wagon upend, Saul and Nedda plunging into the river as the wagon turned atop them. The clawing roots of the giant tree trunk pushed against the wagon, driven by the undercurrent, and Fargo cursed again. He knew full well what the clawing apparition was, knew what rivermen called it, but he found himself thinking about Tom Sprague's warning of deception. It had come all too true.

He turned the Ovaro to try and reach the Graftons where they had disappeared beneath the overturned wagon, and he saw the horses on their sides come up as the harness shafts broke. They swam past him in leaping bounds as they fled in panic. The Grafton's wagon, completely overturned now, was being pushed sideways by the tree trunk under the pressure of the current. In another minute it would crash into Donna's wagon, and Fargo spurred the Ovaro forward through the water with one eye on the wagon and tree trunk as they loomed closer. He reached the horses, took hold of a cheekstrap, and pulled as he heard Donna snap the reins. The wagon rolled, picked up a dozen seconds as the horses thrust forward, but life and death were a matter of seconds now. Flinging a glance backward, he saw the tailgate of her wagon just clear the overturned rig and the tree trunk.

He continued to pull on the cheekstrap of the horse as Donna snapped the reins furiously, and he felt the wagon roll out of the midriver current. He released his grip on the cheekstrap and let her pass him as she made for the bank and he turned to the others who had halted just before midriver. "Wait there," he ordered and sent the Ovaro after the Grafton's wagon which, the roots of the tree still imbedded into it, had come to a halt. He saw Byron Sprague detach himself from the others and ride through the water to the overturned wagon. As Fargo reached the Grafton's converted haywagon, it somehow freed itself from the grip of the clawlike roots and, turned by the current, it floated from midriver to come to a stop where the water grew shallow. Byron Sprague came alongside Fargo as the Ovaro halted ankle deep near the bank. Shedding shirt and Levi's, Fargo plunged into the water. Dimly, he heard Byron Sprague follow him as he swam under the wagon. The water had been muddied, the bottom stirred, but he saw the smashed wagon wheels and some of the wagon's contents spilled into the water.

He groped his way through the murky water, getting a moment of clear visibility as currents carried the silt away, but he found neither Sam nor Nedda Grafton. When his lungs forced him to the surface, he saw Byron Sprague come up at the other end of the overturned wagon. "Nothing," the man said.

"They were carried downriver," Fargo said, certain that Grafton's overweight, hard-breathing body hadn't lasted more than seconds trapped beneath the overturned wagon. Pulling himself from the water, Fargo climbed onto the Ovaro, holding his clothes on the saddle in front of him. He rode back along the bank and entered the river again some fifty yards past where the others waited. He peered into the water until he was satisfied no more unexpected surprises lurked there. When he returned to where the others waited, he beckoned to them. "Cross," he said and moved the pinto onto the dry land of the bank and watched the others start across the river. He had dried himself with a towel from his saddlebag and had his Levi's on before the last wagon rolled ashore. They waited, their eyes on him, and he saw Donna also watching from farther away, the shock still in her broad face.

"What happened? It just came along at the right moment?" Jake Dowd asked.

"Not quite. It was one of three kinds of navigation obstacles that make riverboat captains shake just thinking about them. Riverman call it a sawyer, another they call a planter, and the third one a sleeper. Planters have one end imbedded in the river bottom and they don't move. They reach the surface or a little above it and are particularly dangerous at night. Sleepers are entirely submerged and catch onto deep-hulled boats. Sawyers, this one, rise and fall in cycles, sometimes a half hour apart, sometimes an hour apart. They're the worst of the three because you never know when they'll surface and trap a boat," Fargo said.

"Jesus," Ed Forstmann breathed.

"That was Tom Sprague's warning some true. Deception, symbol of the wild cherry trees, hidden and sudden," Fargo said, his eyes narrowed in thought. Tom Sprague was a man to be reckoned with, not lightly dismissed, a man of complexities. He reached from beyond the grave in more ways than one. Fargo brought the square of paper marked with the number 2 from his saddlebag. It held but a few lines, and he read them to himself in a muttered whisper.

"Go downriver on the north bank to where the cherry trees end. One is marked with an *X*. Your next instructions are buried in front of it."

He pocketed the note and beckoned the others forward. "Follow the river," he said and sent the Ovaro forward at a walk. Donna was first to fall in behind him, and the afternoon sun was drawing to a close when they reached the end of the wild cherry trees. He dismounted and strode along the end of the trees until he found the one he sought, the *X* carved into the reddish brown bark. Using a short-handled shovel from his saddlebag, he began to dig as the others rolled to a halt. He hadn't far to dig before finding a small wooden box, and he pulled it from the earth and opened the lid to see the small square of paper. The neat handwriting was becoming familiar. He took note as he read aloud.

You will follow the river some two miles west, then turn directly north. Stay north and in time you will come to a place called Boulder Mountains. The Shoshoni call this place the trembling land. There are three peaks. You will go to the first one. You must get to the top. If you do not get to the top, the pursuit is at a finish. The trail to the gold ends. At the very top is a tall, pointed rock with a crevice in it. Your next instructions are inside that crevice. It will be a hard climb, I admit, but then great rewards require great effort. That has always been the way of mankind.

Have you ever thought about how nature has equipped almost everything for protection and survival except man? Pliny, the ancient Roman naturalist, put it this way: "To all the rest, she hath given sufficient to clad them, everyone according to their kind: as namely, shells, cods, hard hides, pricks, shags, bristles, hair(fur), down feathers, quills, scales and fleeces of wool. The very trunks and stems of trees and plants she hath defended with bark and rind, yea and the same sometimes double against the injuries of both heat and cold. Man alone, poor wretch, she hath laid all naked upon the bare earth, even on his birthday, to cry and wail from the very first hour he is born into the world."

A truth to think about.

Thomas Sprague

Fargo folded the note away, his eyes narrowed in thought. No idle philosophical musings, Tom Sprague's words. He knew that for certain, now, Fargo told himself. A statement, saying something more than met the eye. Another warning? Perhaps. But for what and of what? Tom Sprague knew the words would burn through him, mocking, an enigma of a message. He moved slowly past the others, Priscilla's round eyes watching him with obvious approval, almost proudly, and he halted beside Donna Sprague. Her face stayed serious, but many things circled deep in the depths of her gray eyes.

"We'll talk later tonight," she said softly, and he climbed onto the Ovaro, then swept the others in a glance.

"Let's roll," he said and walked the Ovaro forward and waved to Byron Sprague. The man rode over to him at once. "Thanks for pitching in," Fargo said.

"Got to try. But we lost and I don't like losing," Byron Sprague said.

"Spoken like a true gambling man," Fargo commented.

"Think we'll find Sam or Nedda?" Byron asked.

"It's always possible. Tell the others to keep a watch as they ride," Fargo said, and the man returned to the other wagons. But no one caught sight of the missing couple, and the day drew to an end before it was time to turn north. A stand of sandbar willow offered a good place to camp by the river, and Fargo called a halt as night descended. They spaced their wagons farther apart than on the other nights, perhaps because the willows invited it, perhaps because the day's events demanded privacy.

Fargo unsaddled the Ovaro, and Priscilla stopped by as he checked the Ovaro's hooves. "It would have been a worse tragedy except for you, Fargo," Priscilla said. "You are a doer of good, a man of righteousness. I knew it that night. Now I know it again." There was not only sincerity in her eyes but a kind of schoolmarm commendation, he felt. He reached out, closed one hand around hers and saw the moment of fluster leap into her face. But she didn't pull away though a faint pink came into her cheeks.

"Nice of you," he said, finally drawing his hand away. Her little smile was hesitant as she turned and hurried away. Priscilla had promise, he told himself. He liked the sound of it. Maybe it would just take time to mellow her, he decided. The others were already turning in, the wagons growing silent, and Fargo strolled to Donna's big farm wagon. She was sitting on a box outside the tailgate, clad in a black nightdress cut low at the top, her large breasts pushing out with fleshy curves.

"Been waiting for you," she said. "If you hadn't helped get my team moving, I'd be with the Graftons."

"They were past saving. You weren't," Fargo said.

"Still, most wouldn't have risked their necks," the woman said and rose to step closer to him. "You deserve a good night on a good mattress."

"Which you happen to have in your wagon," he said.

"Just so happens."

Fargo smiled. "You've no need for this. I accept that you're thankful."

"That's not it, at least not all of it. After what happened I realized that Tom was still being a bastard. He didn't send us on any cakewalk. Maybe I won't make this trip all the way through, and if that happens, I want one more good time, one more good night." She drew a deep breath and her breasts all but overflowed the nightdress. She took his hand and suddenly she was a young girl, anxious and willing, and a mature woman, ready and waiting. The best of each became one as she turned and stepped into the wagon. He followed and enough moonlight came into the wagon for him to see the mattress laid down against one side of the crowded wagon.

Donna dropped to her knees on the mattress and with a slow movement, lifted the nightdress over her head. The large, deep breasts seemed to cascade from her, as though exulting in their freedom. Creamy white and pillowy, each with a large, red circle surrounding a firm, darker red nipple. Donna carried fifteen pounds too much for her, yet she carried it well, flesh still firm and smooth, an abdomen made too convex with a round fold of flesh, but beneath it, her pubic mound smooth and covered with a very thick, very curly, very black triangle that of itself shouted touch me, feel me, enjoy me.

Below the thickly covered mound her fleshy legs seemed to throb with their own earthy sensuousness. Donna was a woman of all sensuality, a woman who avoided boldness by the simple honesty inside her. He

53

came to her, and she reached out, unbuttoned his shirt as he slid off gunbelt and Levi's, and in moments her wide mouth was on his, opening for him, kissing, sucking, a message of lips and tongue. Her large, pillow breasts came against him and she pressed them against his face, her firm nipples growing firmer with the caress of his tongue as he drew their sweet touch into his mouth.

"Yes, oh yes," Donna breathed. "It's been long, too long." She pushed the pillow breasts upward to engulf his face, rubbed them up and down against his mouth, and he reveled in the sensuous smothering. Her hands pressed against his muscled torso, palms flat, moving down his ribs, hips, the sides of his thighs, enjoying every inch of his nakedness against her. "Gorgeous . . . oh, God, so good, so nice," Donna murmured and pushed the rounded softness of her belly against his and gave a small groan of delight. "Yes, yes, oh, God . . . oh, yes," she breathed in a low growl as she found the firm warmth of him and rubbed herself against him. He slid up and down against her, his erectness moving through the dense triangle, pressing down onto the soft mound, and Donna was making coarse, growling noises of animal pleasure, and her hand reached down, fingers clutching for him, finding him and closing around the pulsating shaft.

Her half growl, half scream came at once, and she pushed herself upward, full-fleshed thighs opening and wide hips thrusting upward. Her pubic mound pressed hard against him, and he felt the opened, sequacious lips pressing against him, her warm moistness flowing, the final, ultimate beckoning of the flesh. Tiny, half-growling sounds surged from deep inside her, words finding form in between the groanings of desire: "Now . . . yes . . . yes . . . Jesus . . . now, now."

The moist lips opened wider against his crotch, trying to nibble their way to ecstasy, and he felt Donna's fists pounding against his back in helpless wanting and his own passions skyrocketed. He half rose, came forward, slid into her waiting, wanting moistness, and Donna's moan became almost a deep laugh of pure exultation. Her arms went around him, fleshy body heaving and shaking as she lunged with him, pillow breasts falling from one side to the other as she swayed. "Oh, Jesus . . . ah, ah, aaaaaah," Donna gasped, and Fargo heard the creak of the wagon floorboards under the mattress.

There was no subtle passion, no patient pleasure for Donna Sprague's roaring torrent of earthy release, and he found himself matching her harsh hunger. Her growling explosions of unalloyed, pure carnality were their own kind of cleansing, the past and the future exploding in glory. Finally, as a volcano gathers itself before erupting, her breath grew shorter, came in small bursts of passion that matched her furious upward thrustings against him, and suddenly the world seemed to shatter. Donna's soft-fleshed thighs pressed against him, her body engulfing him, heavy breasts pushed upward into his face. She clung there, everything halted, her very breathing suspended until suddenly, with a tremendous shudder, she breathed again as she fell back onto the mattress and groaned softly.

He stayed in her, kept himself there and heard her small groans of appreciation until finally he withdrew and lay half atop her and saw that Donna Sprague was hard asleep, every part of her relaxed, drawn into a place of new dreams. A tiny smile edged her wide mouth, and asleep in the dim light, she was a young girl again. He lay down with her, his head resting against one pillow breast, and let sleep come to him. Not until the hanging moments before dawn did he wake and pull on Levi's. He saw her eyes come open and stare at him.

"Can't start talk," he murmured, and she nodded in understanding. She sat up, her arms encircling his neck.

"Don't figure I'll be expecting more. I've been around too long for that," she said.

"You never know what tomorrow holds," he said, paused for another moment as her wide mouth closed on his, and then he backed from the wagon. He hurried away, bedded down under a willow some fifty yards away to sleep again until the morning sun woke him. He washed at the river, dressed, and strolled back to the line of wagons. Priscilla stepped from the surrey, buttoning the top of a dark green shirt. She saw him, and he caught the flash in her eyes as she speared him with a combination of anger and reproach. Her back stiff, chin thrust upward, she started to stride past him. "What's got under your saddle?" he asked in surprise.

"Some things are better left undiscussed," she said coldly.

"Such things as what?" he frowned.

"Mistakes. Personal disappointments. My fault. I shouldn't be surprised," Priscilla sniffed.

"At what?" he questioned.

"At being wrong about you. I thought you were different. That was a mistake, I see."

"You're talking in circles. Say it straight," Fargo said and frowned.

Icy disdain formed in her eyes. "I couldn't sleep last night. I went outside and walked some. I passed Donna Sprague's wagon. I hardly think I need spell it out further," Priscilla said.

"And that's what has you all upset?" Fargo said.

"Yes," she snapped. "But then you wouldn't understand."

"I understand you sound jealous, honey," he tossed at her and saw her cheeks flush at once, shock flooding her face.

"How dare you?" she gasped. "I'm nothing of the sort. I'm just terribly disappointed."

"Why?" he asked.

"Because last night was simply inexcusable," she snapped.

"Why?"

"Because you'd no right to wild sexual excesses with Donna last night."

"Why?"

"It was totally improper, completely wrong," Priscilla blazed.

"Why?"

"Stop asking me that one question," she exploded.

"Then talk. What was improper?" Fargo pressed.

"Indulging yourself. Taking advantage of her. A proper person wouldn't have done it."

"I wasn't dancing alone, honey," Fargo said almost blandly.

"Even if she agreed, a gentleman would have backed off. That would have been the proper thing to do," Priscilla insisted.

"Proper hadn't a damn thing to do with it, Prissy," Fargo said and saw her eyes blaze at once. "Let me tell you a little story about being proper. There was a little boy who helped an old lady across the street with a lot of packages. Afterward, she asked him if she could buy him some ice cream and he said sure. Later that day, his ma said to him, 'You didn't help Mrs. Jones to get ice cream, did you?' 'Nope,' he said. 'Then why did you take the ice cream?' his ma asked. 'Because I love ice cream. I never turn it down,' he said." Fargo paused, let her stare back with all the discomfort of mixed emotions racing through her face. "Moral: proper can be a crock of shit, honey," he said. "But it makes a nice shield."

Her lips tightened as she spun and walked to the surrey. He knew she heard his laugh as he walked on to where the Ovaro waited. The others were ready when he finished saddling the horse. "Boulder Mountains," he called and sent the Ovaro forward.

4

Fargo rode within sight of the wagons for most of the morning and saw them slow under the heat of the day. He called a halt at a stream soon after noon and let horses and humans rest for an hour. Priscilla studiously avoided him, he noted, though there was more quiet than anger in her face. She had also unbuttoned the top of her dark green shirt; he smiled inwardly. Harlan and Jerry Brody still stayed close together, and Byron Sprague moved among the others with his easy, pleasant ways. Fargo swung in beside John Dowd as he moved the wagons forward again, his eyes peering at the cracked and splintered Conestoga.

It was the worst of the wagons, but it seemed to still hold up. At least there were no new cracks apparent. "Any sign of Boulder Mountains?" John Dowd asked.

"Not a one," Fargo answered. "We could be looking north the wrong way. I'll be riding northeast and west the rest of the day." He spurred the Ovaro forward and passed Priscilla, who allowed him a serious, unsmiling glance. He moved by the Thiemann wagon and saw their daughter sitting at the tailgate, legs dangling from the end of the wagon. Nothing about her listless personality had changed, and she watched him go by with but a flickering glance, instantly returning her eyes downward to the road. Curiosity made him slow and bring the pinto close to her—curiosity and the fact that experience had taught him that someone apart from the rest on a wagon trail invariably spelled trouble.

"Holding up, Minnie?" he asked pleasantly.

Her eyes went to him, and he saw a kind of veil over them. "Guess so," she said after a long moment.

"Want to ride with me for a spell?" he asked.

Without expression, her face a mask, she answered in almost a monotone. "I don't want to ride with you. I don't want to ride in this wagon. I don't want to be here."

"Sorry about that," Fargo said. "You bothered by leaving some of your friends?" he ventured.

"I don't have any friends," the girl said in a monotone.

"You'll have some after you get the gold," Fargo said for want of a better answer and sent the pinto on with a wave of his hand that wasn't returned. His lips turned grim as he moved forward. Trouble, he muttered to himself. Minnie Thiemann was a potential problem, and he made a mental note to keep a closer watch on her. Putting the horse into a canter, he rode on and climbed into higher land that let him see the terrain in all directions. The rolling land continued so far as he could see—plenty of box elder, quaking aspen and hackberry, high meadows filled with rabbit-brush, corn lillies, and Indian paintbrush to bring color to the land. Bristlegrass and crested wheatgrass gave the horses soft footing, and Fargo sent the Ovaro onto a long ridge that let him scan the land in all directions. He was about to go on when he caught the movement of leaves to the rear, still distant but unmistakable.

The leaves in a long stand of hackberry waved, a steady movement on one level and at one height. Horsemen moving in a line inside the trees, Fargo grunted, his eyes narrowed. They stayed inside the trees, and Fargo felt instant uneasiness wrap itself around him. The line of wagons slowly came into view in the distance, and Fargo's eyes went to the hackberry again. The horsemen continued to stay inside the trees, and Fargo heard the silent curse form inside him. But he watched as the day began to wind to a close, the wagons draw closer, and the horsemen stay in the trees. Uneasiness turned into apprehension and apprehension soon became the edge of certainty. Tom Sprague's words swam from his note: *There may be others who will come after the gold. I was perhaps too loose-tongued one night.*

Fargo continued to watch the distant line of hackberry. The horsemen were being careful to stay inside the tree cover, and that was enough for Fargo. He turned the Ovaro and approached the wagons as dusk began to settle, pulling up in front of the lead rigs. "We've got company that doesn't want to be seen," he announced. "Tom Sprague admitted to having been talkative one night."

"You think they figure to follow us to the gold?" John Dowd asked.

"No, we'd catch onto them along the way and they wouldn't want that. They're going to wipe out most of you and hang onto me until I find them the gold," Fargo said. "I'd guess there are eight to ten of them, and I'd guess they'll wait for everyone to bed down before they hit us."

"Lucky you spotted them," Ed Forstmann said. "Now we'll be ready and waiting for them."

"I want to avoid a pitched gun battle that might get some of you killed. I want an advantage over them," Fargo said.

"How do you figure we can do that?" Sarah Dowd asked.

"You camp, everything as usual," Fargo answered. "They'll be watching. But after you turn in, you sneak out of your wagons and go into the brush. You make a circle around the wagons and lie low."

"When they come in to hit the wagons, they'll be trapped, surrounded," Byron Sprague said. "They'll surrender and we have them."

"Or if they're dumb enough to fight, we'll cut them down. Either way we have the advantage and avoid a pitched gun battle," Fargo said. He gestured to a cluster of bur oak as he turned the Ovaro toward the trees. "Make a loose circle at those oaks and start to camp." The others followed his orders, and he saw Priscilla place the surrey near the Forstmann cut-under Owensboro. The others encamped, made their small supper fires as night descended, and within the hour the fires were put out and the camp settled down for the night. Fargo took his bedroll and set it out near the center of the loose circle. "All right, start crawling out," he ordered in a loud whisper. "One at a time."

He watched as the figures became silent shapes, slipping out of their wagons to crawl into the woods. When they disappeared in a rough circle around the wagons, Fargo lay down on his bedroll and feigned sleep. He estimated that two hours had passed and the silence remained unbroken. They were being very careful. He drew a deep breath and half turned on his side when he heard the soft sound of horses being walked slowly and carefully. He stayed motionless as he let his ears follow the path of the intruders and pulled his eyes open only when the rifle barrel poked him in the ribs. Sitting up, he stared at the horsemen, half of them already dismounted, and quickly counted ten. The one holding the rifle on him was tall and rangy with a scraggly goatee and a gaunt face.

"Well, lookee here," the man said in a hoarse whisper. "This one's out here all by himself. I think we got us the Trailsman, first thing." Fargo pushed to his feet and let his silence confirm the man's words. "I'll keep him covered," the gaunt-faced one said. "The rest of you get in those wagons and start shooting."

Fargo cursed inwardly. The bastards had no qualms about cold-blooded killing. He watched the men move quickly, rifles in hand, darting into the wagons. It was but seconds later that their shouts overlapped each other. "There's nobody in here," one called out.

"Shit, nobody in here, either," someone else said.

"Goddamn wagon's empty," another said, and they were all leaping from the wagons in confusion.

The gaunt-faced one turned to Fargo. "What's goin' on here?" he said, frowning.

"What's going on is that you're surrounded. Drop your guns or you're dead, all of you," Fargo said and enjoyed the fear that leaped into their faces as they exchanged glances. "Drop the guns," he repeated. They looked at the gaunt-faced one, their mouths hanging open, and he stared at Fargo, his lips twitching. "You haven't a damn chance," Fargo said.

The sound was sudden, from his left, and Fargo turned to the Thiemann wagon to see one of the men emerge holding onto Minnie Thiemann. "But we got us a damn hostage," the man shouted triumphantly as he pushed the girl ahead of him, the gun held to her neck. Fargo's eyes fixed on the man holding Minnie Thiemann as the gaunt-faced leader of the group faced the trees.

"Drop your guns and come out or we kill the kid," the gaunt-faced one said, and Fargo silently cursed Minnie Thiemann. She had simply stayed behind in one more show of her bitter, withdrawn inner hostility. Damn her selfishness, he muttered. This time she had put everybody's neck on the line. Fargo's eyes went to the trees, and suddenly Harlan Brody's voice called out.

"Kill the kid. I don't give a shit. I'm not comin' out. I'm gonna blow your damn heads off," Brody snarled, and Fargo saw the men raise their rifles. The man holding Minnie Thiemann cocked his pistol, an old Remington-Beals five-shot single-action piece.

"No, we'll come out," Betsy Thiemann called. "Don't listen to him. We'll come out."

A mutter of voices rose from inside the trees. "Don't hurt the child. We'll come out," Priscilla's voice said.

"Shit, we will," Harlan Brody cut in. Fargo cursed inwardly again. It wouldn't make any difference if they came out. It wouldn't save Minnie Thiemann. They'd kill her anyway, along with the others. In his own selfish way, Harlan Brody recognized that truth. But the tree branches moved. The Thiemanns were coming out. Goddamn, Fargo swore to himself. It was all coming apart before his very eyes. The moment was about to explode in a wild shoot-out, and all because of one self-hating child. He shot a glance at Minnie Thiemann. The gun was no longer pressed tightly against her neck. The man holding her had brought his eyes to the surrounding forest, his gun half turned away to be ready to fire at those emerging from the forest.

It was now or never, Fargo realized, the only moment left when the intruders would still be at a disadvantage. His arm shot out as he flung himself forward, using all the power in his leg muscles to propel himself in a diving tackle. He slammed into the old Remington at the same instant he knocked Minnie Thiemann aside, and he felt the heat against the side of his face as the revolver fired. But as the child went down, his hand closed around the barrel of the pistol and he went down atop the man. He was twisting the gun from the man's hand when the night exploded. He heard the volley from inside the trees, and out of the corner of his eye he saw at least four of the attackers go down. The barrage of gunfire continued as the man tried to wrest his gun free, but Fargo's powerful forearm muscles bulged, and the man gave a curse of pain as his wrist bent backward.

The pistol dropped from his fingers and Fargo brought up a short, whipping uppercut of a blow that landed on the point of the man's chin. The figure went limp, and Fargo pushed himself away, spun in a half crouch and saw the ground strewn with bodies. Gunfire was still coming from inside the trees as four of the attackers were pulling themselves onto their horses to race away. Fargo ran for the Ovaro. The four couldn't be left to escape. That posed too much danger. They'd regroup and start to follow come daylight. They'd choose their spots and pick off the others one by one. Vaulting into the saddle, Fargo sent the Ovaro after the four fleeing riders, two still clearly in sight.

He raised his Colt and saw one of the men turn in the saddle to fire. The Colt sounded first, and the man toppled sideways from his horse. Fargo shifted the gun a few inches, fired again as the second figure tried to swerve and saw the rider slam into a tree as he fell from his horse.

Fargo kept the Ovaro charging through the darkness, the sound of the other two men directly in front of him, and he caught sight of them in but a few moments. They emerged from tree cover to make better time across a clear space, and Fargo holstered the Colt and drew the big Henry from its saddlecase. He raised the rifle to his shoulder as he dropped the reins of the horse and used his thighs and knees to steer his mount. He fired, and the man on the right almost flew over the head of his horse as the powerful rifle slug smashed into him. The other man half reined to a halt and dived from his horse, landed on one shoulder as he hit the ground, and rolled into a line of sagebrush.

Fargo yanked the Ovaro to a halt and leaped out of the saddle, hit the ground on both feet, and dove behind the trunk of a young, thin quaking aspen that was barely thick enough to hide him. A shot followed him and tore a piece of the greenish white bark from midway up the tree. Fargo waited, listening, and heard nothing. The man lay in the sagebrush, biding his time, and Fargo swore softly. The sagebrush was a better hiding place than the lone, thin aspen he crouched behind. The man might be gone if he tried to wait out the night, Fargo pondered, and he slid down behind the tree. He stretched out on the ground, flattening himself on his stomach at the base of the tree trunk and peered across to where the sagebrush formed a thick, low cover.

He stayed motionless and waited and guessed perhaps some twenty minutes had gone by when he saw the movement inside the sagebrush, barely perceptible in the first gray streaks of daylight. For a moment he wasn't sure he had seen correctly, but then he picked it up again, a tunneling movement that disturbed only the top of the brush. The man was crawling on his stomach, hugging the ground inside the sagebrush. Fargo raised the Colt, took aim a few inches in front of the molelike movement of the sagebrush, and fired. A sharp half cry followed, and the sage stopped moving. Fargo waited, but the brush did not move again, and finally Fargo rose and walked to the Ovaro.

It was over, and he rode back to the wagons, not certain of what he'd find and was gratified to see still forms of the attackers strewn across the ground. The others were standing by their wagons, and he saw Ed Forstmann with a bandage around his left arm. "Anyone else hit?" he asked.

"No. They had to fire blindly," Sarah Dowd said, and he saw Minnie Thiemann standing with her parents. She looked away from his harsh glance.

"Anyone want to bury them?" Fargo queried.

"They don't deserve burying," Sarah Dowd snapped, and no one raised a voice in disagreement.

"Then get in your wagons. I'll find another spot to bed down," Fargo said.

"What're you going to do about her?" Harlan Brody asked, gesturing to Minnie. "She damn near got us all killed."

"Abel and Betsy are going to make sure she follows orders," Fargo said.

"We'll see to it," Abel said.

"I will if you don't," Fargo warned and saw Minnie

continued to keep her eyes from him as she climbed into the Owensboro. He turned the horse and led the wagons forward across the field. Dawn had come up, the sky growing yellow-pink, and though none of them had slept, he kept on until the morning was almost over when he found a circle of dogwood that afforded shade enough for everyone. He had just made a spot for himself when Priscilla appeared, a blanket carried under one arm.

"Do you mind if I rest here?" she asked.

"Next to an improper person such as myself?" he returned. "Or have you changed your thinking?"

"I don't know what I think anymore," she said. "I'm still upset about the other night, if that's what you mean."

"Only now you're not sure why," he said, but she didn't answer. She spread her blanket and sat down on it and watched him stretch out.

"Harlan Brody and his brother put their wagon next to mine and they make me nervous," Priscilla said.

"Why?" he questioned.

"They glower whenever they look at me. I've the feeling they think I oughtn't to be here," she said, and Fargo found himself thinking back.

"Remember those four men back in town?" he asked.

"Of course. How could I forget them?"

"Tell me something," Fargo mused aloud. "What if they'd had their way with you? What would you have done afterward?"

Priscilla thought for a moment. "Run, I suppose. Hide. Let the awfulness go away. Close myself away someplace."

"For how long?"

"I don't know. Probably months, maybe a lot longer. I'd feel dirtied, soiled. It'd take time to recover, I know that," she said.

Fargo nodded as thoughts continued to return. They had spoken about combining business with pleasure, but there had been more. *All we gotta do is screw her, over and over,* the one had said. It fit, Fargo thought, frowning. Someone realized that a young woman such as Priscilla would have been devastated. It would have been enough. No killing, no real risks, just a nice, neat way of getting rid of her and having one less to split the gold.

"What are you thinking?" Priscilla asked, her voice cutting into his thoughts. He saw nothing to be gained by making her more nervous about the Brody brothers. Besides, all he had was an educated guess.

"I'm thinking it's time for sleeping," he said and lay back on the bedroll. Priscilla settled down on her blanket, and he saw her studying him, a long, thoughtful appraisal.

"Now who's thinking about things?" he mentioned.

"I'm just wondering," she said, the edge of reproach finding its way into her voice. But something else, also, he noted, a touch of envy, perhaps. He couldn't be sure.

"About what?" he asked.

"Whether Donna's going to be grateful to you for last night," she slid at him, making her tone sound casual when it was anything but.

"Wouldn't know. You just curious or looking down your nose again?" he returned.

"Just a thought," she said and turned on her side, her back to him. He closed his eyes and let sleep engulf him as he heard Priscilla's steady, even breathing.

The warmth of the sun formed a soft blanket, and it was late afternoon when he rose and woke the others.

"We've a few hours travel time left before dark. Let's use it," he said and led the way northward until the night began to descend, and he found a Rocky Mountain maple grove perfect for a campsite. He had just set out his things when Donna paused beside him.

"I was hoping you'd stop by later, but Priscilla Dale's parked her surrey practically on top of my rig," she said.

"Is that so?" Fargo said and felt the smile stay inside him as he thought about Priscilla. Self-protectiveness or possessiveness? The question intrigued him and he let himself toy with it for a moment. Was her armor of properness showing cracks? He let the question hang as he answered Donna. "There'll be other nights," he said, and she nodded with the kind of worldly ruefulness he expected of her. She hurried away, and Fargo undressed to Levi's and gunbelt and took his canteen to fill at a small stream a dozen yards from the campsite. When he finished, he wandered back, skirting the wagons, and he halted when he heard Harlan and Jerry Brody. Closeted inside their wagon, they were conversing in angry tones that clearly carried through the canvas.

"We can't get rid of her tonight," Fargo heard Jerry Brody protest. "It's too risky. She's parked too close to Donna Sprague's rig."

"Then tomorrow night," Harlan Brody answered. "We've got to get rid of some of them. We'll start with her. We paid those bastards in town and they never came through."

"We have to be careful, make it look like an accident," Jerry Brody muttered.

"We'll take care of that," Harlan said, and the two brothers fell silent. Fargo walked on, his mouth a thin line. A question had been answered and a new threat defined. He'd take note of the first and be prepared for the second, he promised himself as he hurried to his bedroll and drew sleep to himself. When morning came, he rose before the others, and when he saw Priscilla, he found himself wondering if her round-cheeked face held a hint of smugness in it.

Her good morning was certainly cheerier than usual, he noted, and when the wagons began to roll, he told them to follow his tracks as he rode on ahead. The land was mostly rolling plains, and it was midday when the character of the terrain began to change. Underfoot, the bunchgrass and the bluestem died away to leave only barren soil, and a few miles farther on the soil began to wear a coating of tiny pebbles. Another hour's ride saw the abrupt rise of Boulder Mountains loom up ahead, the three peaks exactly as Tom Sprague had described them.

But they were barely mountains, Fargo muttered to himself. They were more like very high hills, and when he drew to a halt at the base of the first peak, he saw the tall stone at the top with the crevice inside it. Other than the fact that they were hardly mountains, they were well named, made of nothing but boulders piled high atop each other and scattered in smaller mounds up and down the sides of the peak. Erratic passages wide enough for the wagons to transverse covered the first mountain and led all the way to the peak, each passage bordered on both sides by boulder formations that seemed to rest precariously atop each other. Yet they seemed solid enough, and Fargo waited until the others finally rolled up.

He saw their eyes fall on the treeless, brushless, grassless collection of boulders that rose up before them. He scanned the collection of rocks again as his thoughts turned to the words Tom Sprague had set down. They were no idle examples of learning. Fargo knew better than that, now. But what did they mean? What hidden message had Tom Sprague set forth? He had written about the frailty of man compared to the protective armor with which nature had endowed other forms of life. But what was he really saying? The man had played his little game again, and once more with tantalizing effectiveness. How did his words fit in with the mountain of boulders? Fargo frowned.

Was he warning them to beware of loose boulders? That would make sense. Yet it seemed almost too simple. But Fargo swore silently as he came up with nothing better and saw the others waiting for a signal from him. He scanned the high pyramid of boulders again. There were three uneven paths leading to the top, each surrounded by high mounds of boulders yet wide enough for the wagons to negotiate. They merged into one pathway as they neared the top of the peak alongside the tall stone. "Pick a path and starting climbing," Fargo called out. "Be careful. Don't sideswipe any of the boulders." He started the Ovaro up the nearest path to him and saw Sarah Dowd snap the reins over her team, the first to follow him. The others rolled forward, the Forstmanns rolling in behind Sarah and John Dowd, the Brody brothers and the Thiemanns taking another path. He saw Priscilla move her surrey up the third passage, Donna Sprague moving in a few dozen yards behind. Byron Sprague rode just behind Donna, and Fargo saw Sarah Dowd moving her team faster than the others, obviously excited at the idea of reaching the top of the peak just behind him, Fargo noted.

He let the Ovaro go into a trot, the horse's powerful jet black hindquarters taking the climb with ease. He had reached the midway point when he suddenly felt a trembling sensation, a tremor, at first, then harder, and he was pulling to a halt when the ground began to shake violently. A quick glance told him the others were still urging their wagons forward though Sarah Dowd had begun to pull back. A sharp sound suddenly cut through the air, and the ground shook even more violently. The sharp sound instantly became a series of roaring crashes, and Fargo looked up to see the cascade of boulders tumbling down from above, bouncing off one another in all directions, smashing and crashing their way. He cursed as the Ovaro reared onto its hind legs, and he slid from the saddle as the screams and shouts rose over the sound of the crashing boulders.

"Jump!" he yelled. "Out of your wagons." He barely got the words out when he felt the boulder hurtling toward him and managed to fling himself sideways as the great piece of rock grazed his head. Boulders continued to crash as he heard the sounds of a wagon being splintered and the terror-struck screams of horses. It was suddenly all clear though there was no time to sort it out. There was only time for trying to stay alive. He rose to his feet to see Priscilla on one knee and the boulder coming at her. He dived through the air, slammed into her, and brought her down with him as the boulder hit another rock only inches away. She stayed under him for a moment, her arms clinging to him, and he heard her gasps of breath.

But the ground had begun to stop its violent shaking, and only a few boulders were still crashing aimlessly to the mountainside. Fargo raised his head and gratefully saw the Ovaro standing unharmed to one side, the horse backed up behind a small pyramid of newly fallen rocks. He peered past the horse, across the newly reshaped hillside. The remains of Priscilla's surrey were barely visible under a big boulder, but her horses had been spared, freed when their wagon shafts smashed.

Another tremor shook the ground, and a half dozen smaller boulders fell to one side. Fargo rose, lifting Priscilla with him, his gaze moving across the hillside strewn with boulders still spinning. He watched the figures begin to pick themselves up as he scanned the scene, his lips pulling back as he saw the Dowd wagon. The old Conestoga's cracked frame had been reduced to kindling wood beneath two big boulders. Sarah's leg protruded from below the round edge of one boulder, part of John's arm from beneath the other. Their horses lay crushed beneath the boulders, also, and Fargo scanned the scene as the others began to emerge. Shock clung to their faces, even Harlan Brody without his usual sullenness.

Fargo surveyed the obvious damage and saw the right rear wheel of the Thiemann Owensboro lying in pieces on the ground. Minnie stood near it with no change in her silent, withdrawn manner. A relatively small boulder lay in the middle of Donna's big farm wagon, Fargo saw, and Byron Sprague was climbing carefully over a rock toward him. "What the hell started all that?" the man asked for everyone.

"The movement of the wagons set off the vibrations in the ground," Fargo said. "Tom Sprague said that the Shoshoni call this the trembling land. I know why, now. It's some sort of strange phenomenon, a freak of nature, where any movement sets off violent shocks in the ground. I'd guess these hills are damn near hollow inside, which causes any movement to set off vibrations in the ground. When that happens, the boulders come crashing down."

Fargo paused and swore to himself. The rest of Tom Sprague's note fitted now, also—his discourse on man's lack of natural protective armor all too clear. He had delivered a warning couched as an observation. It was becoming plain that he had taken great pains and perhaps glee to choose challenges where death waited the losers. It was also growing obvious that his cryptic warnings carried as much malicious delight as they did helpful clues. Tom Sprague was becoming a more and more complex man, one in whom a generous challenge now seemed less generous and a good deal more insidious. Abel Thiemann's voice cut into his thoughts.

"What now?" the man asked. "Jesus, I'm afraid to move."

"You should be," Fargo grunted, flashing a quick glance at the boulders at the top of the peak. They appeared deceptively quiet, but he knew that they could be set off by any sizable vibration. "I'd guess that the closer you come to the top of the peak the less it takes to set off another spasm," Fargo thought aloud. "So we're going to move back down, very, very slowly."

"I've an extra wheel, but we've got to get it in place," Abel said.

"We'll do that, but we work very slowly," Fargo said.

"My wagon's finished," Priscilla said.

"But your horses are all right. Collect whatever personal things you can and you'll ride one and have a pack horse," Fargo said. "And move slowly."

"What about the Dowds?" Ed Forstmann asked.

"There's nothing we can do. I don't think we can move those boulders, and if we did, it'd certainly set up vibrations," Fargo said. "The rest of you start backing your wagons downhill, real slow. Stay on foot and lead your horses." He watched as Priscilla began to go through her things inside the smashed surrey and the Brody brothers began to lead their team down the hillside. "I'll get that damn boulder out of my rig after I get to the bottom," Donna Sprague said as she followed. Myra Forstmann came next and found space enough to turn her wagon while her husband began to help the Thiemanns replace their rear wheel. A tremor ran through the hillside at one point but quickly stopped, and Fargo joined the others in a deep breath of relief.

The sun had begun to near the horizon when the Thiemann wagon had been repaired and slowly rolled to the bottom of the hill. Fargo was the last to reach the bottom, leading the Ovaro with him, and he halted to peer up at the top of the peak. The last of the sun still touched the tall stone with the crevice in the center, and Fargo's eyes moved across the mound of boulders just below it. "What are you thinking?" Ed Forstmann asked, following his gaze.

"I'm thinking this search is over unless we can reach that peak," Fargo said.

"Seems all we'll do is get ourselves killed trying.

We get closer to the top and we'll be sending more of those boulders down on us. You said so yourself," Betsy Thiemann said.

"The wagons would surely set off the vibrations. A horse would probably do it, and anyone near the top would sure as hell be crushed to death. But maybe there is a way," Fargo said. "One person, moving very carefully on foot, might reach the top."

"Without getting killed?" Myra Forstmann asked. Fargo's shrug was its own kind of answer.

"You're thinking of trying it," Priscilla said.

"I got paid to do a job. That still holds," Fargo said, and Priscilla stepped closer.

"You don't have to do this, not for me. I'll forget the gold," Priscilla said, her round eyes full of earnest honesty.

"I won't," Harlan Brody put in, his voice a growl.

"It's too dangerous," Priscilla said.

"Thanks, but I got paid to do a job. I don't take to going back on an agreement. I'm going to give it a try come morning. There's a chance it can be done," Fargo said and turned to the others. "You'll bed down here. This is pretty solid ground, but let's not take any chances. Move slowly, pick a spot, and stay there."

He watched them turn away, Harlan Brody's face back to its normal sullenness, the others unable to hide the hope in their eyes. Except for Priscilla. She followed to where he set down his bedroll, her blanket under one arm. "I want to stay here," she said, and he nodded. If Harlan Brody still held any thoughts about her, he'd have to wait for another night. Fargo shed clothes, down to his shorts, and Priscilla managed to don the blue robe with modesty. But as he lay stretched out, he saw her come to kneel at the edge of the bedroll. "You saved my life up there. That boulder would've crushed me," she said.

"I was at the right place at the right time," he said.

"Maybe, but that doesn't change what I feel," she said. "Or what I'm beginning to understand."

"Such as?"

Her eyes moved across his torso, lingered, her face grave. She leaned forward, and suddenly her lips touched his, softness that clung for a moment, a tentative kiss, and then drew back. "Such as things about myself, about being grateful and being proper," Priscilla said.

"You understand about liking ice cream?" Fargo smiled, his hand holding her shoulder.

"I'm working on it," she said. "I need a little more time."

"Time might be a luxury for you, for all of us," Fargo said, and her face remained grave as she lay down on her blanket.

"I know," she murmured. "Good night, Fargo."

"Keep working on it," he said and let himself stay awake a little longer and found his thoughts not on wide-eyed young ladies with new awakenings, not even on the danger of boulders poised to descend, but on Tom Sprague. Once again, Fargo felt the malice wrapped inside the strange games the man was playing as, from beyond the grave, he manipulated the lives of others. It almost seemed as though he were punishing as much as offering. Fargo realized he had become a paid player, bound as much by his own principles as anything else. It was clear Tom Sprague had counted on that, too. Fargo's small smile was tight. The man had been a master of craftiness. Closing off thoughts, Fargo let sleep come to him, finally.

5

The dawn woke him, and he moved slowly as he washed and dressed. Patience, he murmured to himself, and he was peering up to the top of Boulder Mountains as the others woke. A thin layer of morning mist still clung to the peak, and he became aware of Donna's eyes on him. "Good luck," she said softly, and he nodded in return. Priscilla had risen, the robe wrapped tightly around her slender shape, her eyes filled with concern. Fargo took in the others as they emerged from their wagons, some clothed, others only half dressed, his gaze brief and hard.

"You stay here, no matter what you hear or see," he said. "You can't be helping me except by staying here." Byron Sprague nodded, and Fargo paused at Priscilla's side. "Hold onto the Ovaro. I don't want him following me," he said, and Priscilla moved at once to get the horse. Fargo turned and began to walk up the mountainside. The trailing ribbons of mist still formed a gauzelike wrapping around parts of the slope, and he took one of the paths the wagons had used. As the sun grew stronger, the mists evaporated, except for those still clinging to the top, and Fargo circled slowly past the mounds of boulders newly formed.

When he reached the spot where stray sticks of the Dowd wagon protruded from beneath the two great boulders, he slowed his pace further. He climbed past the spot and had reached a few dozen feet higher when he felt a tremor course through the ground. He halted, frowning at once. He had been moving slowly, each step taken with cautious pressure, and he swore in dismay. He'd been certain he'd been careful enough not to cause any vibrations. Yet the tremor had been all too real. A bad sign so soon in his climb, he thought, grimacing. He pushed gently against a mound of boulders as he started to move on again and felt one move ever so slightly. Taking another careful step, he climbed on, skirting through small crevices between mounds of boulders. He glanced up the mountainside. The mists had all but dissipated, but the new mounds of stone blocked out much of everything except the peak and, spotting a passageway between towering pyramids of rock, he resumed his climb.

He had gone perhaps another ten minutes, testing the ground with each step before moving on, when another tremor ran through the top of the mountain. The tremor suddenly became a steady trembling, and then the sound of a boulder rolling downward. Fargo swore as he pressed himself against a tall slab of rock and stayed unmoving, hardly daring to breathe. The lone boulder stopped rolling, but the trembling on the ground continued. Finally, when it grew less, Fargo risked moving again, and he tested each step as he climbed, being certain to cause no sudden pressure. He used a sliding motion as he climbed in an effort to decrease the impact of each step when suddenly the trembling increased again. Fargo halted, cursed silently, unable to understand how he could be causing the vibrations as he wondered whether it was suicidal to go on.

The trembling continued and Fargo halted alongside a pillar of boulders already precariously poised. He stayed motionless, not moving a finger, and frowned as the trembling grew stronger. He couldn't be causing the vibrations, he thought, not with his unmoving silence. Did the trembling feed on itself? Once started, did it gather its own strength? The questions still dangled in his mind when the trembling suddenly escalated and he heard the sharp sound of rock striking rock. The sound suddenly magnified as boulders began to cascade down from the peak. Fargo's eyes darted across the rock-strewn mountainside, and he spied a tall slab of granite with an overhang barely large enough for one person. He streaked for it as the ground shook violently now, accompanied by the thundering crash of falling boulders and then, suddenly, another sound, a sharp cry.

"Jesus . . . oh, damn," he heard the voice scream and then break off in a cry of pain, repeated, then suddenly cut off by the crash of a boulder that shook the mountainside again. It took Fargo a moment before he recognized the voice as Jerry Brody's, and then he reached the narrow overhang as a shower of boulders rained past him. Jerry Brody's voice came again, a spiraling scream of pain, and then it ended again with the sound of another boulder smashing its way downward.

Fargo lay flattened under the narrow overhang, hands over his head, and heard only the sound of the crashing boulders as they bounced their way downward to come to rest in new pyramids across the face of the mountainside. Jerry Brody's voice had come from above him, perhaps a few hundred feet higher, and as the ground stopped trembling, the boulders halted their crashing descent. Fargo cursed softly as he lifted his head and shook rock dust from his shoulders. It was all clear now. He hadn't set off the vibrations, not alone, not with the caution with which he had moved. Jerry Brody had been closer to the peak, hurrying, perhaps scrambling his way upward in a stupid, heavy-footed race to reach the peak. Other facts were becoming clear. He had to have started a little before dawn and his stumbling progress certain to have set off the first wave of vibrations. It was then only a matter of time before his progress had inevitably triggered the rest of what happened.

One more certainty presented itself: Jerry Brody hadn't thought up the attempt on his own. Harlan had put him up to it. Stupid, greedy fools, both of them, Fargo muttered inwardly as he pushed to his feet and began the climb again. He moved even more slowly, now, pausing between every sliding step as tremors still coursed through the ground. The mountainside, not unlike a nerve that had already been made sensitive to pain, lay ready to convulse again at any moment. Fargo felt as though he were literally walking on eggs as he continued the precarious climb.

When he had taken almost an hour to go a few hundred feet more, he paused as he saw Jerry Brody's body lying facedown on the slope. One boulder lay across the middle of his back, crushing his spine. Another had smashed into the rear of his head. The trembling mountain had said this far and no farther. Jerry Brody had taken his last climb, and Fargo's mouth was a thin line as he moved past the spot. The earth trembled again, harder, and Fargo halted and realized he was perspiring heavily under the heat of the sun. The tall stone at the peak seemed an unattainable goal as the earth tremors continued.

Fargo waited till they grew less, and then he settled onto his hands and knees to distribute his weight more evenly as he began his climb again. It had its effect and the tremors subsided altogether. But Fargo fought away the impulse to hurry. There was no place to hide as he neared the peak and nothing to hold back the boulders that would rain down on him if the mountainside erupted again. Pausing every few moments to listen and feel the earth, he moved upward, staying on his hands and knees. It seemed a terrible distance though only another thousand feet and finally the peak loomed up in front of him, and he felt his shirt soaked with perspiration. But the earth had not trembled and, using a section of protruding rock, he pulled himself to his feet.

The tall stone with the crevice inside it beckoned to him, and he stepped forward and reached into the cut, the rock scraping against his arm. It was firm, no shaking to it, and he let a breath of relief escape his lips. He groped along the sides of the narrow crevice, felt only the rock and then, as he lowered his hand, he touched the side of a leather pouch. His fingers finding one edge, he slowly drew the pouch through the crevice and into the open. Small and flat, it folded easily in half, and he pushed it into his pocket and turned away from the peak. He'd not take time to look inside it here. It was too dangerous. Something unexpected could set off the vibrations. It wouldn't take much, and he glimpsed a half dozen vultures wheeling over the place where Jerry Brody lay.

The heavy birds swooping in to land at one spot

could be enough to set off a tremor that in turn would set off another tremor and instantly the shaking would gather force. Fargo pushed the flat leather pouch deeper into his pocket as he lowered himself to the ground and began to slide downward. Again, he forced himself not to hurry and cursed as he saw the circling flock of vultures come lower. But their piercing vision had seen him, a living creature moving below, and they swept upward at once. They wanted no part of the living. They would wait, circle endlessly and wait, winging with a macabre awareness that their prize was already won.

Fargo continued to slide downward, maneuvering around piles of boulders, pausing when a tremor ran through the earth for a moment. Glancing back, he saw the vultures start to descend again, and he took a chance as he moved faster down the mountainside. Finally, as the flock of huge birds came in to land, he rose and began running. The ground trembled almost at once, but he was almost at the bottom of the mountainside, and he saw Priscilla waving him on as the tremors subsided. He came to a halt where she waited, and the others moved closer at once. But Fargo's eyes were the cold blue of an icy pond as he stepped toward Harlan Brody.

The youth's darting eyes narrowed as he saw Fargo come at him. "It wasn't my idea," Harlan Brody said.

"You're a damn liar," Fargo flung back. "Why didn't you tell me he'd gone up ahead of me?" Harlan Brody didn't answer, and Fargo's left lashed out in a lightninglike blow that caught Brody on the side of his jaw. The youth went down at once. "You almost got me killed, you son of a bitch," Fargo rasped. Harlan Brody shook cobwebs from his head, pushed to his feet, and lunged forward with a snarl. He moved with surprising quickness, but Fargo parried his blows, stepping backward as the youth roared in rage.

"I've had it with you, Mister Trailsman," Brody snarled, then tried two fast left jabs and followed with a swinging right hook. Fargo parried the jabs, side-stepped the right hook and brought up his own short left uppercut. The blow caught Brody on the side of his jaw, enough to make him half stagger. The youth tried to avoid Fargo's following short right and failed. The blow snapped his head back and Fargo's left hook sent him sprawling. Harlan Brody tried to lift his head, but fell back, half-conscious, and Fargo's eyes were still hard as they swept the others. Their glances reflected renewed respect, and Fargo started to draw the flat leather pouch from his pocket when Priscilla's voice pierced the air.

"Look out," she cried, and Fargo had neither the time nor the need to ask questions. The big Colt was already in his hand as he spun and saw Harlan Brody, still on the ground, yanking the pistol from his holster. Fargo fired, and Harlan Brody's pistol flew from his hand as he cursed in pain. Fargo stepped to the pistol where it lay on the ground and saw the chamber had been shattered. Holstering the Colt, he turned to Harlan Brody, his voice cold steel.

"You got your brother killed. You draw on me again and you'll get yourself killed," Fargo said. Harlan Brody rose to his feet, holding his numbed hand, his sullen anger cloaked in fear. But that would pass. Harlan Brody would find a time to strike back, some-how, someway. He'd have to do so for himself. It was part of his character. He'd still need watching, Fargo grunted to himself, and he turned to the others as he drew the flat leather pouch from his pocket. Harlan Brody had halted to listen, he noted, and Fargo began to read aloud.

> If you have come this far, and have this in hand, I congratulate all of you. I confess I am curious as to how many of you have fallen. But I am admirous that some of you, at least, are here. On the other side of Boulder Mountains there is a long road. At one point it will narrow. At the end of the narrow part you'll find a long, hollow log.
>
> Look inside the log. Take heart. You have made real progress. You are nearing your goal. But I leave you with a riddle. When is a road not a road?
>
> Tom Sprague

Fargo reread the note in silence, his lips pursing in thought. It was different than any of the previous ones. No scholarly discourse this time. It offered encouragement. It dangled the prize again, the promise of riches just waiting to be attached. Sincere exhortation or more malicious cleverness? Fargo turned the thought in his mind as he admitted that he'd become suspicious of Tom Sprague's generosity. And the riddle had to have its own special meaning, he realized. One thing was clear. Tom Sprague had not finished toying with those who had come to take his offer.

Fargo pushed the note into his pocket as a long glance at the others told him they were waiting to go on, their faces carrying the determined eagerness of those who were committed to easy riches. Only Priscilla's round-cheeked countenance held a hint of uncertainty. "We'll be going around Boulder Mountains and that'll take time. Let's get moving," Fargo said and climbed onto the Ovaro. Priscilla swung onto one of her horses and pulled the other along, heavily saddled with packs and bags. The others followed, Harlan Brody falling into line behind the Forstmann Owensboro, and Fargo rode on ahead. He gave the now-silent mountains of boulders a wide berth, and he just reached the rear edge of the formation when dusk began to descend.

He found a stretch of bur oak and made camp, setting out his bedroll as he chewed on cold strips of beef jerky. He was undressed down to his underpants when he saw Priscilla approach with her blanket. "Good. I was coming to get you," he said and caught the moment of pleased surprise in her eyes. "Not for what you're thinking," he said chuckling.

"I wasn't thinking anything," she said, instantly proper, but her eyes lingered on his body as he took a length of thin cord from inside his saddle pack.

"A new bond between us," he said as he looped one end of the cord around her wrist. "Settle yourself before I tie the other end to me," he said. Frowning, she set the blanket down and lowered herself onto it. Somehow remaining modest, she turned the blue robe into a covering sheet and watched Fargo fasten the other end of the cord to his wrist.

"What's all this about?" she asked.

"I'm going to be sleeping hard. It's about nobody making off with you while I'm asleep," Fargo said. "Such as Harlan Brody."

"You think he'd do that?" Priscilla asked.

"You'd be one less to share the gold with," Fargo said. "And he tried it before." He let the words hang as he watched the frown slide across her face, then deepen as her thoughts pulled themselves together.

"Those men back in town," she breathed.

"Bull's-eye," Fargo said and lay down on his

bedroll, the cord stretching limply to Priscilla's wrist. "Get to sleep. No one's going to bother you without my knowing it."

"Thank you, Fargo. That's all I seem to be saying these days," Priscilla offered.

"It'll do," he said, turned on his side, and let tiredness sweep over him. He slept quickly and woke three times during the night as he felt the cord on his wrist pull. But each time it was Priscilla turning in her sleep, and when dawn came, he woke again and looked across at her. The robe had come partly off to show one long, lithe and beautiful leg, deliciously curved, tantalizing bent at the knee. He rose, used his canteen to wash, and he was dressed as Priscilla woke and sat up, pulling the robe around her at once. She brushed her ash blond hair back with one hand and looked disconcertingly lovely. She caught the appraisal in his eyes at once.

"What are you thinking at this early hour?" she asked.

"I'm thinking that modesty is like being proper," he said, and Priscilla frowned back. "It makes a good shield," he finished, and she looked away, but there was no stiffness in her this time. She went behind the trees to dress, and Fargo saddled the Ovaro while the others got up. He found Donna beside him as the morning sun rose.

"You wondering why I'm not upset about Jerry? After all, he was kin," she asked.

"No. You already told me there was no love lost among you," Fargo answered.

"That's right. He was a fool and fools seldom change. I'm glad you came out of it all right," she said. "Be careful of Harlan. He's a fool, too, but a dangerous one."

"I'm sure of that, but thanks for the advice," Fargo said. She returned to her overloaded rig, and he waited till the others were ready to move before setting out. He found the road at the back side of Boulder Mountains, and it was both long and winding, as far as the eye could see, and he rode on ahead. The road continued to wind its way past stands of Rocky Mountain maple, quaking aspen, box elder, and alligator juniper. There were long, open land stretches that became heavy with tree cover miles later, and the day went into midafternoon and the road still stretched its winding way.

The sun had begun to slide toward the horizon land and the road reached beyond a line of serviceberry when, in the distance, he saw a wall of granite rise up high into the air. He squinted, peering ahead as he rode closer and saw that the road went on right through the smooth stone wall. But he saw something more and drew to a halt at the edge of a deep chasm that ran the entire length of the land from north to south. Only a single, narrow bridge of land, an extension of the road he had just traveled, led to the other side. He sat the Ovaro quietly, his gaze moving back and forth across the narrow bridge of land over the chasm and finally, when the others rolled to a halt, his eyes went to the wagons. He measured with his eyes, returning his gaze to the narrow bridge of land. It was just wide enough to accommodate the width of the wagons with perhaps six inches of room on either side.

But then Tom Sprague would have known that, Fargo murmured silently. Was he challenging their skill as well as their daring? Fargo frowned at the question. Such a challenge might have been enough for most men to offer but not Tom Sprague. It was too ordinary, devoid of deception, and far too simple for him. But then the others had seemed devoid of deception, also, Fargo reminded himself, and he stared at the narrow bridge of land. The riddle in the note came into his mind. *When is a road not a road?* Did it somehow fit here, he pondered. He turned the riddle in his thoughts and came up with no insights, and he was still searching his mind when Betsy Thiemann's voice cut into his musings.

"We can do it," she said. "It'll be touch and go, but we can do it. It'll just take being real careful."

"It seems that could do it," Fargo agreed. "And it seems too simple. I'm bothered. I want to explore some before you start across."

"We don't need to wait," Harlan Brody said.

"We'll wait," Ed Forstmann said.

"Us, too," Betsy Thiemann chimed in, and Fargo turned the Ovaro onto the narrow strip, the chasm a sheer drop on both sides. He kept the horse at a slow walk, directly in the middle of the road, his eyes scanning first one side and then the other. The narrow strip stayed the same. The wagons would have their six inches of clearance on each side all the way across it seemed. It was almost zero tolerance, yet he was grateful for small favors, he told himself. They could do it with skill and extreme caution if their luck held out. But it still seemed too even a test for Tom Sprague, and the nagging stayed inside Fargo, the riddle still refusing to fit. He was still wrestling with his misgivings when he spied movement in the middle of the strip some fifty yards in front of him.

The movement became a shape sliding its way toward him on the ground, and Fargo swung from the horse, moving quickly but carefully. Landing on the balls of his feet, he dropped the reins to the ground, and the Ovaro halted. Fargo took a dozen quick strides to confront the snake before it drew any closer to the Ovaro. "Shit," he muttered as he saw a big bull snake, some eight feet long and twenty-five pounds in weight, he guessed. No venomous reptile, the bull snake was a constrictor with plenty of bite. But to the horse it would be a big snake and that would be enough. If the Ovaro reared up and swung his rump around, he could go off one or another side of the road, so Fargo lengthened his stride.

He halted before the snake, blocking the Ovaro's view of the reptile, and waved his arms. The constrictor halted, opened formidable jaws and hissed, but didn't lunge. Fargo kicked out at it, and it drew its head back, waited, poised to attack again or take flight. It was not a terribly aggressive snake and would rather retreat if it had a chance. He drew his foot back, moved slightly to one side, and kicked out at the series of dark blotches that covered its yellowish skin. The bull snake drew back again, and Fargo aimed another kick at it with one foot and stamped hard on the narrow strip with the other. He came forward as he saw the constrictor start to move sideways, and this time his kick caught the snake just about in its middle. The snake whipped its body around as it attempted to flee, lunged sideways, and then drew back as it became aware of the edge of the narrow strip. It was still drawing back when Fargo saw the ground crumple along the length of the edge, falling away with startling suddenness and taking the snake with it.

With a frown of surprise Fargo watched the snake plunge downward with the crumpled length of earth, and he stared silently at the spot for a long moment. He pushed away, jumping to conclusions as he strode back to the Ovaro but his frown grew deeper as he fished into his pack and drew out a short-handled spade. Stepping carefully, he moved to another stretch of the narrow strip, knelt on one knee, and reached out with the spade. He used the flat side of the tool to strike hard against the edge of the strip. The ground crumpled away at once, falling into the chasm in clumps.

He moved sideways, halted at another stretch of the narrow strip, and hit the ground again with the spade. The earth gave way instantly, and Fargo rose and walked to the other side of the road. He hit at the edge with the spade and the ground broke off and tumbled into the chasm. "Goddamn," he muttered. Both sides were exactly alike. Both sides fell away at any pressure. It was all making sense now. Tom Sprague had not offered a simple challenge of skill. The sides would have given way at the weight of the wagons. At least one would've gone over, taking horses and passengers with it. Maybe more than one, Fargo grunted. The riddle revealed itself, too. When is a road not a road? When it's a death trap, when it can't be used, Fargo muttered and strode back to where the Ovaro waited. The center of the narrow strip of land stayed firm but the center was too narrow for any of the wagons.

Fargo moved the Ovaro backward, carefully guiding the horse, until he reached the firm land where the others waited. "You saw it," he said. "The edge won't hold, not on either side. You'd go over. The firm land doesn't give you enough clearance."

"What do we do?" Myra Forstmann asked, her eyes moving up and down the length of the chasm that seemed without end. "We can't go around this. Besides, the other side's straight rock. The only way is on that road the cuts through it."

Fargo's lips thinned. She was right. "You'll have to leave your wagons and go on horseback. Riding single file, we can make it across," he said.

"Leave all our things?" Donna frowned. "I don't like that."

"Me neither," Abel Thiemann agreed. "Anybody coming by could just go off with everything. Indians could take what they fancy and torch the rest."

"It's a chance you'll have to take," Fargo said.

Harlan Brody's angry voice cut in. "You'd like that, wouldn't you, leaving us with only the shirts on our backs."

"What's that supposed to mean?" Fargo snapped.

"It means I think you're enjoying everything he's done so far. It means you haven't done enough for us," Brody shouted.

"You're right about the last part. He's been very clever," Fargo conceded.

"Maybe you'd like none of us left so's you could get the gold," Brody accused. "Well, it won't happen that way. I'm going across and I'll make it."

"Don't be a damn fool," Fargo said.

"We go fast enough the edges will hold. You just watch me," Harlan Brody said and snapped the reins over his team. The horses sprang forward onto the narrow strip, and Brody lashed them again with the reins. "Git up, git up," he shouted and the horses responded. Fargo watched the wagon race along the narrow strip, jouncing crazily as the wheel rims slipped on the right edge of the road. More of the soil crumpled away, but the wagon somehow stayed on enough firm ground to keep going. It was halfway across the narrow road strip, still outrunning the ground that crumpled away under the wheels, when suddenly the left rear wheel skidded. Fargo grimaced as he saw the wagon go sideways, its weight pulling the front end and the two horses with it. Harlan Brody's screaming curse rang through the air as the horses and wagon toppled over the edge.

Fargo looked away and swore silently as the screams of the horses mingled with Harlan Brody's voice until it all came to an end in the terrible crash and abrupt silence that followed. Fargo waited a long moment before he turned to the others. "Once a damn fool always a damn fool," he said quietly. "Any of you still want to take your wagons over?" No one answered, and Fargo took the harshness out of his voice. "With any luck you can come back to your wagons after you get the gold," he said. "Now unhitch your horses, gather your personal gear, and use one horse each as a pack animal."

He saw Byron Sprague dismount and begin to help Donna, and Priscilla came over to wait beside him. "I've been thinking about Tom Sprague," she said. "At first I thought he was offering us a chance to get the gold, making us work for it. But now all it seems is that he's offering us a chance to get killed trying."

"It's beginning to look more and more that way," Fargo agreed. "But then he did hire me to help you."

"And put your neck on the line, too," Priscilla said, and again Fargo nodded agreement.

"Maybe he's just too damn clever for the rest of us," Fargo said, voicing a thought he had quietly considered earlier.

"We're ready," Abel Thiemann's voice cut in, and Fargo cast a glance at the gathering dusk. It was lowering too quickly, and he made a quick decision.

"Spread out and find a spot to bed down. We'll stay here for the night and cross in the morning," he said, turning to Priscilla. "With Harlan gone you won't have to be bedding down next to me," he mentioned.

"That's so," she agreed and walked off to unsaddle her horses. Night soon slid across the land, the chasm turning into a black space, and Fargo spread his bedroll between two flat rocks where a lone hackberry grew at an angle. He had undressed when the figure appeared and lay down the blanket. Priscilla settled herself only inches from his bedroll and caught the amusement in his glance. "I've always been quick to form habits," she said.

"But not quick to be honest," he commented.

Her round eyes stayed on him. "All right, one for you," she murmured. "I like being next to you. I like looking at your body. Honest enough?"

"A definite improvement," he said. "What if I found us a special spot to camp tomorrow night?" he asked.

She paused before answering. "Find it," she said after a moment. "That's more honesty, I guess."

"You guess?"

"Honesty doesn't always translate into action, not with me, and not in some things," she said.

"I'm sure of that," he said.

"Then you won't be disappointed," she said.

"I don't expect to be disappointed," he told her. "Just keep being honest."

"All right," she said, and he heard the firmness in her voice. It was the only good omen he'd come upon during the whole damn trip so far.

6

"Walk your horses and stay in the center of the road," he told everyone else in the new morning light as he started across the narrow bridge of land, the Ovaro following behind him. He moved cautiously, testing each step, when he reached the middle of the passage where Harlan Brody had gone over the edge. But the narrow strip remained firm at its center, and he finally reached the other side where the towering wall of stone rose up. The road stretched out ahead through the huge stone walls and he scanned the ledge to find the long, hollow log to the right, resting against the base of the stone wall.

He was beside it, on his knees and reaching one arm into the log as the others came up. He felt nothing, then rose and stepped to the other end where he reached deep inside again. This time his hand curled around a rolled-up length of parchment, and he drew it from the log to see it was tied with a piece of twine that he quickly opened and unrolled the parchment. Tom Sprague's penmanship was neater than usual, the words scrolled with the flair of a wide-tipped quill pen.

Congratulations, again:
    You have only one more note after this. You have done

remarkably well, better than I had expected. You will continue to follow the road through the high rock. When it ends, you will head northwest toward the Missouri River headwaters. Just before you reach the headwaters you'll find a large stand of cottonwoods that runs west for almost a mile. Enter the cottonwoods and continue west till you reach the end of them where you'll see two of the trees that have grown together. At the base of this double tree you'll find a mark and a hollow behind it. There you'll find your final instructions.

Do you know that the cottonwood tree is a specie of poplar? The poplar is an interesting tree with some forty species. Even more interesting is its name. Legend has it that the name has come down from the Latin of the ancient Romans. They so liked to use the poplar as places for their public meetings that they called it the *arbor populi*, the people's tree.

We have so much to learn about today from yesterday.

Tom Sprague

Fargo let a wry sound escape his lips. Once again, Tom Sprague had returned to seemingly innocent observations of casual scholarship. But it was not at all that, Fargo knew. It was very planned, made of carefully hidden meanings as had been the other ones. But what meanings? Fargo swore silently as the words were only words to him, offering nothing but a further example of Tom Sprague's cleverness. He put the note into his pocket, mounted the Ovaro, and waved the others on. The road that cut through the high walls of rock led on for miles to end only when the huge rock formation came to an end. A high plain followed, and the sun grew hot. Fargo slowed the horses to a walk as he continued to ponder the note in his pocket, wrestling with its cloaked meaning.

When the day neared an end, he had found no key

to the note, and he halted at a thick grove of service-berry with wild plums mixed in along a series of low hills, an ideal spot to make camp. He let the others find their own spots, and after they had finished their meals, he called them together. "Maybe I could figure out more on the notes if I knew more about Tom Sprague," he said. "Tell me about him. You all knew him. You first." He nodded to Ed and Myra Forstmann.

The couple exchanged quick glances before answering, Fargo noted. "We can't tell you much. He kind of passed through our lives. We saw him only at a few family affairs," Ed Forstmann said.

"I know some of what he did, his prospecting and school teaching. I want to know if he was happy or depressed, a man who liked people or didn't. Did he talk about anything in particular?" Fargo questioned.

"He didn't talk much," Myra Forstmann said. "As Ed mentioned, we didn't know much about him."

Fargo turned to the Thiemanns, very aware that the Forstmanns had given him quick, dismissive answers. Abel Thiemann met Fargo's gaze with a half shrug.

"He was an ordinary sort," Abel said flatly. "Nothing much to tell about him."

"Yes, very ordinary," Betsy agreed, too quickly, and Fargo saw her chin lift, stubbornness in it, almost defiance.

"That's all you can say about him?" Fargo queried.

"That's right," the woman said. "He was real ordinary." Fargo turned from her, his eyes passing over Minnie Thiemann when the girl's voice cut in.

"They hated Uncle Tom," she said, and Fargo's brows lifted.

"You be still, you miserable little child," Betsy Thiemann snapped at her daughter.

"Well, it's true. You always said so. I heard you," Minnie insisted, and Fargo saw the woman's hand come up to strike, but she pulled it back, her face white with anger.

"You stop making up things, you hear me?" Betsy Thiemann shouted at the child. "Either you don't say anything or you lie and make up things, that's all you do."

"I didn't make up anything," Minnie Thiemann snapped back and then fell silent, but Fargo saw the half smile of triumph touch her face before it lapsed back into its usual expressionlessness. Had the child been telling the truth, he wondered. Or had she simply seized a chance to embarrass her parents? He turned away, certain there'd be no admissions of anything from Abel or Betsy Thiemann. Byron Sprague was next, a waiting smile on his sharply angled face.

"Tom Sprague never approved of my way of life or my philosophy," he said.

"Win big or lose big?"

"That's right. That just wasn't in him. It was foreign to his way of thinking. Consequently, we were never very close," Byron said.

"So you've not much to tell me," Fargo said.

"I'm afraid not. I was surprised to have been included in this venture," the man said.

"Why do you think he included you?" Fargo queried.

"Perhaps because he included everyone who was family and I qualified on that ground," Byron said.

Fargo's eyes went to Donna. "You ought to be able to tell me something about him," he said.

"Being married to someone doesn't always mean you know them," Donna said, and Fargo smiled. The remark was a truth and also an evasion.

"Maybe so, but give it a try. Did you argue a lot? Did he hold a grudge, or was he the kind to forgive and forget? How did you part, on good terms or bad? Give me something about his character," Fargo said.

"He liked being alone a lot. I don't know why he ever got married. He didn't seem to care much one way or the other when we broke up. I tried to make him happy, I really did. He was always more interested in being a schoolteacher than a husband," Donna said.

Fargo's lips pursed. She was giving him answers of only surface information that revealed nothing about the nature of the man, and he saw he'd do no better by pressing her. She was too contained to be tricked or rattled. Priscilla was last, and he turned to her.

"Confession time," she said simply. "I never knew Tom Sprague. In fact, I wasn't even invited. It was my mother he invited. But she'd been terribly ill for years and bedridden. I decided to go in her place, get some of the gold, and use it for doctor bills."

"Thanks," Fargo said dryly, sweeping them all with his glance. Priscilla was the only one he believed. She had been honest, albeit a little late. But the others had all seen fit to cloak their part of the truth, for whatever their reasons. None of their answers satisfied. Tom Sprague might have been many things, but ordinary wasn't one of them, and it was unlikely he was a man who didn't talk much. In his experience Fargo had found that a man as good with a pen as Tom Sprague was as likely good with his tongue. Minnie Thiemann had cast a shadow on all her parents had said, which was not very much in the first place. Donna had been smoothly evasive, and Byron had a weak answer for being invited by a man who disliked him.

Fargo had learned nothing from them that would in any way help him decipher Tom Sprague's note, and as darkness fell and the others prepared to bed down, he took his bedroll deep into one of the low hills. As he did, he circled to pass Priscilla and paused beside her. "Watch where I go and follow as soon as the others are bedded down," he said.

"If I don't get lost," she murmured.

"I'll find you," he said and walked on under an almost full moon. He climbed and found a thicket with a little clearing surrounded by serviceberry and set down his bedroll. Moonlight came in through an opening at the top of the trees to bathe the thicket in a pale but nonetheless strong light. He undressed down to trousers, and the night stayed warm as he left the thicket to make his way out into the brush of the hillside. He crouched down on one knee, still thinking about the note in his jacket and his frustrating inability to decipher it. The wait was not a long one when he spied the figure moving through the tall grass, coming toward him in an uncertain path.

He gave a low whistle and saw Priscilla change direction and hurry forward. He stood up and she saw him, came to him, and he reached out and took her hand. She said nothing as he led the way into the thicket, but he noted that she held the blue robe tight around her. She halted, her eyes taking in the soft circle made almost magical by the pale silver light. "Cozy enough?" he asked.

"Too cozy, perhaps," she said.

"Change of heart?" Fargo asked.

"I don't know. Maybe just misgivings."

"Why?" he questioned.

"I'm not sure. Doesn't everyone? . . . the first time?" She shrugged.

"Is that what this is?" Fargo asked.

"Don't tell me you didn't guess that," Priscilla said.

"Some things I never take for granted. I've been fooled before," he said. "And no, not everyone has misgivings the first time."

She was silent for a long moment. "I wonder," she said, finally.

"You wonder what?" Fargo asked.

"Are they better off for it? Or am I?" she asked, as much of herself as of him.

He smiled. "A good question and one I sure can't answer," Fargo said. "But maybe you can," he added, took her hand again, and placed it on his chest. She didn't pull away, and he took his hand down after a moment. Her palm, flattened against his chest, moved slowly across the smoothness of his pectorals, across his shoulders, then down his chest again, onto the flatness of his abdomen, and he saw her lips come open. Moving slowly, he lay back onto the bedroll, gently pulling her with him, and she came down beside him on both knees. He unbuttoned his Levi's, then took her hand again and guided it gently against his belly, almost down to his groin until she pulled away.

"No, oh, no," she gasped, fright in her voice, but her mouth was open, and she was breathing hard. His hands went to her shoulders, closing around them inside the blue robe, feeling their rounded smoothness. He moved his hands, pushed against the fabric, and the robe fell from her shoulders and dropped to her waist. He felt her shudder. He took in a slender torso and breasts beautifully full and high, a milky white hue to her skin, and each breast tipped by a small, flat, cherry red nipple plainly virginally untouched. His hands still holding her shoulders, he found her mouth with his, pressed, gently at first, then harder. "No . . . oh, oh . . ." she murmured, but there was only breathless pleasure in her tone and he pressed harder.

Her lips came open, softness flowing to him, and he let the tip of his tongue explore, a quick caress, and Priscilla's hands tightened against him at once. "Oh, oh," she gasped, but she stayed, not pulling back, and suddenly her lips were working, responding to his mouth, nature ignoring her hands that had become small fists pressed against him. He drew her closer, and as her breasts came against his chest, she shuddered at the touch. His hands slid from her shoulders to cup around the milky white breasts, and she uttered a sharp cry, but her own tongue continued to dart out, the flesh answering with its own will. Her hands rose, pressed against his, holding his fingers to her breasts until he pulled away and she gave a sharp cry of disappointment.

But when he pushed the rest of the robe away, she gasped again, a sound fashioned of apprehension and wanting. He saw a flat abdomen, a tiny dot in the center, slender hips and a slightly convex little belly that narrowed to a triangle of shockingly dense bushiness where tiny black tendrils were outlined against the milk whiteness of her thighs. It was a strangely disconcerting contrast, every other part of her pristinely virginal, her every tentative touch, the long, smooth as cream legs, the cherry red, flat nipples, and then the dense, black triangle that fairly shouted sex with waiting abandon.

Priscilla stared as he pulled her down beside him, his hand cupping one breast to slowly smooth a path under the full, high cup and around the cherry-tip areola. He caressed gently, letting his thumb move slowly back and forth across the flat nipple, and suddenly it was no longer flat, forming itself into a tiny peak that reached upward with sweet eagerness. He brought his face down, held it against the soft-firm mound, and Priscilla uttered a soft moan as he let his mouth find the cherry red tip, and the moan became a cry of delight. He drew the soft mound deeper into his mouth, let his tongue circle the areola, and felt the thin, soft hairs that surrounded its edges. "Ah . . . aaaaah," she sighed, and her hands were suddenly moving through his hair, sliding up and down the back of his neck. "Oh, God . . . oh my God," she breathed. "So good . . . so nice."

She pushed his mouth harder around her breast, and he felt her legs moving, sliding back and forth against each other even as they remained tightly closed. When he pulled his lips from her breasts, he saw that she stared, eyes round and wide, as though she couldn't believe what was happening. He brought one leg up to lie half over her. "Oh, oh, God," she immediately cried out, and her palms pushed against his chest as he moved a hand downward across her stomach, tracing a simmering pathway, paused at the tiny indentation, and then slid lower. He felt her stiffen again, every part of her growing taut and he paused, his hand staying against the curve of her belly.

She lay as if in suspended motion for uncounted seconds, and then he felt her relax and a tremor course through the long, lovely body, and he moved his hand again, ever so slowly. The tautness didn't return, but when his hand slid to the bushy triangle, she cried out, alarm in her voice, and he heard the edge of panic come into it. "No, oh, no . . . oh, no, please," she gasped, and he let his hand stay, unmoving, pressed firmly against her. His voice was a whisper against her breast.

"Should I stop? Whatever you want, Priscilla," he said. "You tell me."

The silence only seemed forever. When the answer came, the single word was barely audible. "No," she breathed. "No." There was only gentle understanding in his smile as he trailed his hand slowly, pushing through the dense triangle, thickets of black, filamentous whorls, strangely exciting as they strayed out to lie on her smooth thighs, and he pressed against the swollen pubic mound, rubbed his hand on it, and Priscilla's fists were making thudding little sounds on the bedroll. Fargo moved through the bushy triangle, his fingers reaching the bottom edge, and he felt the touch of dampness. Priscilla's legs moved, again held tightly together, pressed hard against each other and his probing fingers. But Fargo's touch stayed gentle as he slid his hand between her smooth thighs. Priscilla half screamed and, legs still pressed together, her hips lifted, fell back, lifted again, and her legs moved up and down as they held together, as if in a rehearsal of desire.

He pressed deeper between her thighs, slid upward toward the black triangle, and Priscilla's gasps grew quicker. Suddenly he moved quickly, up to the tip of her softness where her thighs were moist. She screamed and clutched at him, and as he pressed further, feeling the lubricous folds, she burst into a cry of release, and her thighs fell away from each other.

"Oh, yes, yes, yes, yeeesss . . ." she screamed and continued to scream as he caressed deeper, exploring the honeyed walls, and now her long lovely legs were moving from side to side, seized with aimless abandon, and in her cried all the wondrous pleasure of discovery.

He moved and brought his own excitement atop her, and at the touch, she screamed with new delight. Her legs grew stiff, fell away, then closed against his hips. He took her hand, brought it to him, held her there, and Priscilla's eyes were closed as she screamed and closed her fingers around him. "Oh, oh, migod, migod, oh, yes, yes, oh wonderful, oh, I like, I want," she said, flinging out words, and suddenly she was moving under him, bringing her hips forward and pulling at him, and he let her bring him to the portal of pleasure. Her scream was muffled against his chest as she encircled him with arms and legs and her body working, bucking, thrusting, trying to find his gift, and when he slid into her, she continued to scream in total rapture against his chest.

The last vestiges of properness had shattered into a thousand unwanted pieces, replaced by flaming passion, but he moved slowly, gently, and heard her cries fling aside the last of apprehension. Her smooth honey glove clasped around him, thoroughly exciting, the eternal caress of the eternal dance. Her transformation was more than sudden, more than a slow awakening, but an explosion of the senses that was all the more surprising because of the past. But he was immersed in his own pleasure, enjoying what he had brought and what she gave in return, and he moved with gentle rhythm in her. Priscilla's eyes were closed now, her ash blond hair tossing wildly as she turned her head from side to side, hands clasping and unclasping against him as ecstasy discovered and overwhelmed the very senses it fed upon. "Yes, yes, so good, oh, God, so good," she murmured, and her body rose and fell with his every plunge until she was one with him, bodies fused together by the fire of ecstasy. She virtually hurled herself against him with each scream of pleasure melting into the last.

It was with slow suddenness that he felt her body change its rhythm, her stomach drawing in, pelvis moving downward, holding for a long moment, and then her hands were digging into his back. "Something . . . something, oh, God, now, now," she screamed, and her head arched backward, the veins of her neck standing out. He let himself release with her as he felt the wonderful contractions around him, pulsations of eternal pleasure created to be forever transient. Her lovely body shuddered and trembled, and her cries were made of mournfulness as well as pleasure as the moment of moments exploded away and finally she sank back, legs still clutched around him. "Too much . . . oh, God, too much," she breathed and her wide, round eyes stared at him for confirmation.

"Always too much," he agreed. "And always never enough."

She kept her legs around him, and he stayed with her, the embers of throbbing pleasure still clinging until finally her thighs fell open and she uttered a long sigh as he moved to lie beside her. She turned and brought one breast against his lips. "It was more wonderful than I'd ever expected," she said. "I'm sure you had a lot to do with that."

"We try," he said.

"Modesty doesn't become you," she sniffed. She

pushed herself against him and let out a long sigh. "I've never been so beautifully tired," she said, and it seemed only seconds when he heard the sound sleep in her breathing. He closed his eyes as he smiled. Priscilla had been an unexpected mixture of sudden contrasts, the kind of awakening one always wants to see but seldom finds. In a way she exemplified the trip. Nothing had been as he'd expected there, either. He uttered a grim snort as he let sleep come to him with her in his arms.

7

He woke before daybreak and shook her gently until her light blue eyes opened to stare up at him, blinking slowly. "Remember me?" he asked.

"Oh, yes, indeed," she said and sat up, the high, round breasts swaying beautifully together as she reached for the robe.

"Best get back," he said. "No sense in causing talk."

"Definitely not," Priscilla agreed and rose, wrapping the robe tightly around her. She paused, her eyes moving over his muscled nakedness. "Don't wait too long," she said.

"For what?"

A tiny smile touched her lips. "To find another spot for us," she said.

"From Miss Proper to Miss Passionate," he remarked.

"All your fault," she said tartly and hurried from the thicket. He rose and watched her until she disappeared at the base of the hill. Returning to the thicket, he took in another hour of sleep and rose when the sun filtered through the trees. The others were awake and ready to ride when he joined them, and he took the time for a breakfast of wild plums before setting westward toward the Missouri River headwaters. The ride was long, combining steep hills and rolling plains, and he set a slow pace to conserve the horses.

As he rode, he spent most of his time pondering Tom Sprague's note, going over it sentence by sentence as he sought the hidden meaning he was certain it held. *Arbor populi,* the people's trees, the Romans had called the poplars. But the Romans were no longer around, and the poplars were no longer the people's trees. They never had been over here. So what was he saying, Fargo asked himself. Was he saying that the cottonwoods would afford them the kind of comfort and welcome they had the Romans? Fargo threw aside the thought. It was far too benign for Tom Sprague. He taught deception and unpleasant surprise wrapped in history lessons.

Fargo's eyes narrowed. Perhaps Sprague was saying that they wouldn't find the poplars the trees the Romans had favored for their public meetings. That was more in keeping with the thinking of his proven deviousness, Fargo pondered. Then why would the cottonwoods be different for them, he asked. Why wouldn't they be welcomed for public meetings as the Romans had welcomed them? That made little sense either, Fargo thought, grimacing. Trees don't change their character. Fargo swore silently as the enigmatic words continued to elude explanation.

When dusk began to descend, he found a small pond surrounded by a forest of Rocky Mountain maple and had everyone unload their packhorses for the night. He had finished his meal of beef jerky and the night lay over the land, when he found Priscilla at his side, her round eyes grave. "I thought I could wait. I was wrong," she said.

His eyes scanned the denseness of the maples, and he rose and took his bedroll. "Never keep a lady waiting," he said, and she hurried alongside as he went into the forest. He'd gone perhaps a quarter mile when he found a circle of spineleaf moss and set his bedroll out on it. He sat, started to shed clothes, and Priscilla came down beside him.

"I don't know myself. I don't understand myself, the way I feel," she said.

"How is that?"

"So . . . so consumed," she said. "So shameless . . . so bold."

"It's called discovering yourself," Fargo said. "Some gals are more honest about it than others. It's especially strong when it comes all at once."

"You mean after being so held in," she said, and he shrugged. "That's over. God, is it ever," she said. Her hands reached out, and she was pulling the last of his clothes from him. "I want more, to know more, learn more, feel more," she said and, with a wriggle, slid out of the robe, and he saw the pride, almost defiance, in the light blue eyes as she proudly enjoyed his admiration. He reached out and drew her to him. In moments his mouth tasted of first one high breast and then the other.

Priscilla groaned and pressed her breasts deeper into his mouth, and Fargo felt the cherry red tips grow again, rise to meet his tongue, and in moments Priscilla tossed and turned half beneath him and groaned in pleasure. When he drew back and let his hand begin to trace a lambent line down her abdomen, she moved, half turned, and he felt her reach down, groping until she found what she sought. "Oh, migod . . . oh, oh, yes, yes," she gasped out, her hand closing around his vibrant warmth. "Oh, let me, let me," she murmured as she stroked, gently caressed, explored and cradled, bringing her face down, and little breathless gasps of joyous discovery came from her. She turned, still clutching him, and rubbed her body up and down against his muscled smoothness, pressing him into her dense, jet pubic mound, and her lovely, smooth legs came up to straddle him as she moved back and forth. She pressed, explored, savored each motion, and as the throbbing, pulsating warmth of him beckoned, she gave a cry of exhaltation as she brought her roscid portal to him and plunged forward.

"Ah, ah, aaaaaah," she moaned as she rose and fell over him, twisting her hips, determined to fill every inch of herself with his pulsing rhythm. She had become a wild thing, ash blond hair tossing in every direction, gasps and groans falling from her lips, the full, high breasts bouncing, and with all a magnificently extravagant beauty. She had indeed been transformed, and she reveled in every second of it. She fell forward, breasts pressed into his face, and her cries gathered into spiraling screams even as the contractions inside her spiraled. He felt himself erupt with her, swept up by the headlong passion of her, and she trembled against him, lithe legs pressed hard into his sides.

Finally, with a terrible dismay, her cries of rapture broke and became almost a whimpered plea. "No, no . . . too soon, too soon," she murmured against him as for the second time, she learned that ecstasy was evanescent. She lay atop him, tiny tremors still coursing through her as she held herself hard against him. Finally, her smooth-lined legs straightening, she fell from him, and he turned to lay half atop her and watched the high, round breasts rise and fall with every deep breath. "Should I be ashamed of myself?" she asked, sounding terribly young and innocent.

"Try proud," he said, and she smiled, liking the sound of it. Her arms coming around him, she turned and settled into almost instant sleep. He relaxed beside her. For the second time, the trip had taken on certain pleasant aspects that seemed certain to stay. Perhaps it was a good omen, he reflected, then closed his eyes and let sleep sweep over him until the waiting hour just before dawn. She woke with him and pulled the robe on.

"Tomorrow night?" she asked.

"Depends on the place," he answered.

"Try," she said and hurried away. Fargo lay back on the bedroll. She wasn't suddenly turning possessive. He'd detect that at once. She was simply a kid with a new toy, her own awakening. Enjoying that with her would bring its own special pleasure, he knew, and pulled sleep around himself. The morning came with a simmering sun, and he set a fast pace while the day still held a measure of coolness. By midday he had slowed, and he rested the horses at a small stream surrounded by peachleaf willows. He sat against one of the furrowed, black barks and rested until Donna appeared beside him.

"Went looking for you last night," she remarked.

Fargo kept his voice casual. "I bedded down in the maples. Anything special?" he asked.

"Thought we might spend the night together," she said. "I've been wondering if you've forgotten the night we had."

"No, of course not," Fargo said.

"I'll come by tonight, then," the woman said.

"No," Fargo said quickly and saw Donna's eyes study him.

"I'll have to find a spot, first, and that'll depend on where we camp," he said hastily.

"I suppose so," she said, and he pushed to his feet.

"Time to move," he said and Donna nodded.

"Find a spot," she said and walked to where she'd left her horses. Fargo climbed onto the Ovaro and silently swore at the problems of unexpected complications. Priscilla wouldn't be put off, not with such hungry eagerness inside her. He swore again and put the horse into a trot. The land opened up and, despite the heat, they made good time. He skirted Crazy Peak and knew they'd make the headwaters by the next day. He scanned the land, veered to his right, and waved to the others to follow, then cut across a long, flat open stretch of land as the sun descended. When he called a halt to camp, it was on an almost barren plateau where everyone bedded down in clear sight of each other.

He offered Donna a helpless shrug, and she allowed a wry half smile. "That's life," she said. "I've learned how to wait." He nodded and moved away to unsaddle the Ovaro. The moon had come up when Priscilla appeared at his side with her blanket, a pout on her round-cheeked face.

"This is really lousy," she muttered.

"I agree. Nature doesn't always cooperate," he said, placatingly. "I'll try to do better tomorrow." Priscilla settled onto her blanket as her pout stayed. He glanced across the flat land and saw Donna standing, watching Priscilla settle onto her blanket. Fargo shed clothes and turned on his side on his bedroll, very aware of the value of delaying tactics and certain he'd need luck as well as imagination come tomorrow night.

He slept quickly and soundly and had everyone in the saddle before the morning sun cleared the horizon. By midafternoon the Missouri River headwaters were only a few miles ahead. He felt the excitement gathering inside him but not with uneasiness. The note in his pocket remained an enigma. The land grew suddenly harsher, becoming a place of sharp drops and hidden arroyos, unexpected box canyons and small draws all mixed in with stretches of level land.

The cottonwoods rose up in sight, covering the flat land as well as draws and ravines, growing in thick profusion, and he slowed the Ovaro to a walk as he entered the forest. The note in his pocket suddenly throbbed, and uneasiness became apprehension. His sixth sense pulled at him, and he drew to a halt and let the others come up to him. He peered into the forest that stretched out in front of him, deep and silent, and his lips were a thin line. "I'm going to scout ahead," he said. "The rest of you walk your horses, real slowly, stay together and stay quiet. No talking."

"You see something?" Abel Thiemann asked.

"It's not what I see, it's what I feel," Fargo answered.

"I'm going to talk," Minnie said sullenly.

"Minnie doesn't mean that," her mother said hastily.

"Yes, I do. I don't want to be here. I won't do anything you want," Minnie said.

"She talks, gag her and tie her hands," Fargo said and moved the Ovaro forward. He saw the concern in Priscilla's eyes as he rode past her and on into the forest. He rode the horse at a fast walk and threaded his way through the heavy-twigged limbs of the poplars as he peered hard at the trees. The question again pushed at him as he rode. What hidden message was Tom Sprague sending by telling them how the Romans loved to meet under the poplars? There had to be one, Fargo thought. Tom Sprague hadn't suddenly changed colors. Fargo kept the Ovaro moving through the heart of the forest as he pondered, swearing silently in frustration.

He had gone perhaps another half mile, he guessed, when he reined to an abrupt halt and felt his nostrils twitching. The odors that drifted to him were both familiar and alarming as he took in fish oil and bear grease. He slid from the saddle at once, left the Ovaro's reins draped over a low limb, and hurried forward on foot. The odors grew stronger and Fargo dropped into a low crouching lope as he moved forward, dropping to a halt on one knee as the figures took shape in front of him. A quick count showed ten braves, bodies shiny with bear grease, the fish oil making their black hair shine. Two dragged a big black-tailed deer behind them with rawhide thongs tied around its antlers.

A brave riding a mottled white pony wore a soft buckskin shirt, and Fargo took in the circular designs embroidered on it. "Northern Shoshoni," he grunted to himself. The Indians were moving toward him when they drew to a halt and Fargo heard the sounds from his left, turned, and saw another band coming through the trees. Six more, he counted, three of them with red fox pelts tied to their waists. They exchanged shouts of greeting, and the second band came to ride in the same direction, some fifty feet from the others. All carried a mixture of short bows with rawhide quivers for their arrows and army carbines, undoubtedly tokens of victory.

It was equally clear that they used the forest for hunting, and suddenly Tom Sprague's words took on their real meaning. *Arbor populi,* Fargo murmured silently, the trees the people loved for their meetings. But no Romans now. The Northern Shoshoni were the people meeting in the poplars. Fargo rose and began to move with silent steps back to where he had left the Ovaro. Had he not decided to ride on ahead, his sixth sense coming to the rescue again, they would all have blundered head-on into the Shoshoni. His lips were pulled back in a grimace as he reached the Ovaro, pulled himself into the saddle, and moved the horse at a fast walk.

The Shoshoni were traveling casually, yet he guessed they were not more than ten minutes behind, and when he caught sight of Priscilla and Byron Sprague, he waved frantically at them. They halted at once, and the others came up as Fargo swung down from the Ovaro. "Shoshoni, coming this way. Get your horses as deep into a thicket as you can. Then get back here with your rifles," Fargo said. The others scattered, following orders at once, and Fargo led the Ovaro into a space between two thick-branched trees. The others wouldn't find complete cover for all their horses, but he'd have to make do with whatever they managed. Yanking the big Henry from its saddlecase, he ran to where the others came into view, stumbling their way toward him. "Take cover and wait till I shoot, then open fire. Not a sound until they get within close range. If we bring down enough of them, the rest will hightail it," Fargo said. "Now pick a place and keep your head down." He dropped behind the broad trunk of the nearest tree and saw Priscilla lying on her stomach, a Winchester in her hands and a Remington pocket pistol tucked into the waistband of her skirt.

She disappeared from his sight, and he brought his eyes back to the forest. With a good opening volley and a good dose of luck they might bring it off, he told himself, and his eyes peered through the trees. He caught the sound of them first, branches being brushed back, then guttural exchanges, the sound of ponies snorting. The two groups were still riding fifty feet from each other. The largest one would pass at his right, the other to his left, Fargo saw, and he raised the big Henry to his shoulder. The big buck wearing the shirt came into view, then vanished behind a broad tree trunk.

Fargo waited, his finger resting on the trigger, when the scream cut through the air. "Over here, they're over here," it came, Minnie Thiemann's voice sharp as a knife, ripping apart the one chance for survival. He cursed the child in bitter fury as he fired. But the Shoshoni were already scattering, and Fargo saw them send their ponies to both sides and begin to charge forward. Priscilla and the others were firing, but their shots were wild and Fargo rose as the shrill cries of the Shoshoni attack filled the forest.

"Get your horses. Run for it. Find cover someplace," he shouted. The command was pitifully inadequate, he realized, and he heard Minnie Thiemann's wild laughter over the shouts and curses and wished he could find her in his sights. He glimpsed Ed and Myra Forstmann climbing onto their horses, and he turned and ran to the Ovaro and leaped into the saddle. Priscilla had disappeared from his line of vision, and he swung the pinto in a half circle to duck away from three arrows that hurled past his head. The Shoshoni were in full attack, both bands, firing rifles and arrows, and Fargo pushed the Henry into its saddlecase and drew his Colt.

A near-naked form flashed in front of him, and he fired. The Shoshoni fell from his pony. Another brave whirled into sight, racing headlong at him. Fargo ducked a shot from the Indian's carbine, fired the Colt, and saw the man's forehead disappear. Fargo whirled the Ovaro again and sent the horse streaking through the trees as two arrows thudded into a poplar inches away. He searched the forest for Priscilla, but didn't see her and heard the shouts of the Shoshoni in pursuit of someone.

He turned the horse in pursuit when three braves swung in close behind him, and he made another turn, sharp to his right, and down a short slope where he found himself on a ridge of half-clear land. He put the pinto into a near gallop and slowed almost at once as two more Shoshoni appeared directly ahead of him. Colt in hand, he fired, and the nearest figure threw up both hands as he toppled backward from his pony. Fargo swerved, left this time, and the other brave's arrow sailed past him. But the trio at his rear were closing fast, and he sent the Ovaro down another slope only to rein in abruptly as he saw a sharp drop into a ravine cut off his path. He turned, raced along the bottom edge of the slope, and caught sight of a pathway leading upward. He took it at once, the high-pitched war whoops of the Shoshoni echoing through the trees.

Their pursuit had begun to take in a smaller area, and Fargo cursed, aware that it meant that Priscilla and the others hadn't been able to scatter far enough. A bullet snapped a young branch in two just over his head, and he ducked, glanced to his left, and saw the Shoshoni charging at him. Firing as he dug heels into the Ovaro's ribs, his first shot missed but his second caught the Indian in his shoulder and the man pitched sideways in pain, lost control of his horse, and fell to the ground. Fargo swerved again and tried to cut through an opening in the cottonwoods when three more Shoshoni darted from the trees to block his way. Cursing their moves, maneuvers made by men who knew every inch of the forest, he changed directions again, painfully aware that he was being boxed in.

He fired off two more rounds and one of the trio cried out in pain as he clutched his abdomen and fell forward against his pony. He stayed bent over the horse until he toppled from it, both hands still pressed against his midsection. But three shots and two arrows whistled past Fargo's head from three different directions, and Fargo crashed the Ovaro into a dense thicket. Pulling to a halt, he leaped from the saddle, reloaded, and saw the Shoshoni slow, one halting, as they peered into the thicket. Two sent their horses to the left while three others continued to search the thicket with narrowed eyes, arrows poised on their bows. One near-naked rider came up alongside another, and Fargo's finger tightened on the trigger. The Colt fired, moved a fraction of an inch to the left, and fired again. Both men toppled from their ponies, hitting against each other as they fell.

The third Indian ducked and swerved his horse away just as Fargo heard the sound of the two horses crashing through the thicket behind him. He whirled, ducked away from an arrow that grazed his hair, ran under the Ovaro's head, and came up firing. The Shoshoni flattened himself onto his pony. Fargo dived for the Ovaro, vaulted into the saddle, and sent the horse crashing out of the thicket. He saw three more Shoshoni converging on him and plunged down the side of the slope, turned when he reached the edge of the ravine, and let the Ovaro walk a precipitous pathway along the narrow, flat ledge of ground. Overhanging cottonwoods kept the Indians from getting a clear shot at him, and he saw the end of the ravine come into sight. He was almost at it when a tomahawk whistled down from above.

He felt it crash into the side of his head, a grazing blow yet enough to make the world spin. He shook his head, tried to clear away the gray veil that had dropped over him, and managed to see the two Shoshoni on foot, rushing down the slope at him. He raised the Colt, fired, missed, and the grayness swirled around him again. He was still trying to clear his head when he felt the blow smash into the top of his skull, another tomahawk, this time landing more directly. He knew he was cursing, falling from the horse, and he was still semiconscious as he hit the ground. Another blow slammed hard into him and, from a faraway place, it seemed, he heard voices and felt the pain of more blows, and suddenly the world came to an end. Consciousness, perhaps life, he realized in a last, fleeting second, had left him.

8

A fact was born. New knowledge made itself known. Breath was not the first sign of life. Sensation spelled the difference between the living and the dead. The thought not so much a thought as a dim awareness. The side of his face hurt. The dead did not feel pain. The realization hung inside him, prodding, demanding recognition, and slowly he pulled his eyes open. The world took on shape, wavy lines at first, then objects finding form, rocks, trees, the steep side of earth that was the ravine. Fargo turned onto his side and felt wetness against his face—sticky, thick, blood on its way to coagulating.

Suddenly everything pained him—face, arms, shoulders, back, ribs, legs, and he lay still for several minutes, his breath coming in long, painful gasps. Finally he pushed to a sitting position, fighting off the waves of pain that swept over him. He sat and listened to the silence and knew the immensity of the gratefulness that wrapped itself around him. Memory returned, and he saw himself being flung over the edge of the ravine. They had left him for dead and gone on, and now he slowly pushed himself up, swayed, fell against the side of earth, then stayed there until his balance returned. He spied a small stream that ran crossway to the ravine and made his way to it, dropped to his knees, and carefully washed the blood from his face. Letting the cool of the water bring new strength to his pain-wracked body, he rested until finally he pushed to his feet again.

He craned his neck at the earth wall of the ravine and saw enough protruding rock and sinewy brush to offer a path to climb. He began slowly, carefully, fighting down the pain of his body, using the tough brush to hang onto and the small ledges of rock as a foothold. He found he had to rest after every few feet, and bruised skin and muscles cried out in protest. But he finally reached the top, rested again, then pulled himself over the edge to lay drinking in deep draughts of air. It was only after he regained his breath and rose to his feet that he realized the Colt was still in its holster. He reloaded, moved into the trees, and whistled, then heard the Ovaro coming toward him.

He held the horse by the reins as he walked through the edge of the trees, searching the ground, first spotting two of the horses. Ed Forstmann lay near one, Myra near the other, both riddled with arrows. Fargo peered at the surrounding land, his eyes following the unshod hoofprints where they circled and dug into the ground. He came upon Donna next, her face almost unrecognizable, and, his lips tight, he walked on, again following the hoofprints. Abel Thiemann came into sight, pinned against a young sapling with a half dozen arrows through his body. Betsy Thiemann lay on the other side of the sapling, her clothes pulled from her. They had enjoyed her before splitting her skull with a tomahawk.

Fargo moved on, scanning the ground again until he came onto Byron Sprague. He had been killed by two arrows that pierced his neck. "Win big or lose big," Fargo murmured, bitterness coating his voice. The hoofprints grew scattered, some in a straight line, others dug in deep where the ponies had reared and then surged forward. He searched to his left and to his right, retraced steps and circled back, seeking two more victims and finding neither. He turned and followed the Indian pony prints as they finally came together and formed a double line of riders. Finally, with a leap of hope, he spotted the two sets of footprints following the last of the Shoshoni ponies. They had taken Minnie Thiemann and Priscilla.

He climbed onto the Ovaro and began to follow the trail as it led from the forest into a long draw and through a stand of quaking aspen. Priscilla and Minnie Thiemann were both young enough to be taken prisoner. The Shoshoni took only the young. They would enjoy Priscilla as long as it pleased them and then either cast her aside, broken and emptied, to be used as a slave by the squaws, or do her in. Minnie Thiemann would be raised and trained in the Shoshoni ways, young enough to make into a Shoshoni woman.

He had not understood the depth of Minnie Thiemann's problems, he realized. He had thought of her as a spoiled, sullen child full of rebellious attitudes who needed to be taken in hand and disciplined. But what she had done only a few hours ago had not been an act of immature rebellion but an act of hatred, hatred of her parents and probably of herself. Minnie Thiemann had made everyone pay for her tortured, twisted inner sickness. He blamed himself for not having recognized the depths of her problems as he quickened the pinto's pace through the aspen. He rode for another hour when he slowed, the sounds drifting through the trees to him, voices, men and women and the high-pitched cries of children.

The Shoshoni camp lay directly ahead, and he cast a glance skyward to see the gray of dusk beginning to spread over the land. Dismounting, he led the Ovaro behind him until he saw the camp stretched out beside a stream. He tethered the horse to a low branch and went forward on foot until he dropped down behind the trees where he had a close view of a large main camp with at least five tipis, a longhouse, and racks for drying and stretching skins. He quickly spotted Priscilla, bound to a stake near one of the tipis. Her blouse hung open, the high, round breasts exposed, and a half circle of old squaws poked at her with long, bony fingers, more in curiosity than in malice.

He surveyed the rest of the camp and finally saw Minnie Thiemann. Untied, she followed a young brave, her hand resting lightly on his arm. When he paused to gather sticks, she helped him and again rested her hand on his arm as he walked to one of the tipis. Fargo was still frowning when his eyes returned to Priscilla. The old squaws had left her, and she had slumped to the ground, her wrists over her head where they were tied to the stake. He saw despair mixed with the anger in her eyes as the gray of the sky quickly deepened. The Shoshoni were commencing their night meal, and Fargo saw the Indian with the buckskin shirt step from one of the tipis and take the wooden bowl of gruel a young squaw brought to him.

Fargo rested behind the trees and scanned the camp again. There were no sentries. The Shoshoni felt secure and confident, and Fargo took comfort in that. They'd not be posting sentries nor have the camp on alert. Dusk was rapidly turning to dark, and Fargo sat back against a tree trunk as he watched the Shoshoni finish their meal. No one offered Priscilla anything, he noted, but Minnie Thiemann was given food as she sat close beside the young buck. There was something in her face he had not seen before. She looked happy. He wished he could feel some shred of sympathy for her, but her twisted selfishness had caused the deaths of six people. He knew he was coming close to making an uncomfortable decision about Minnie Thiemann.

The Shoshoni finished their meal, and the brave in the buckskin shirt retired to a tipi at the far end of the camp. Most of the squaws entered a tipi only a few yards from where Priscilla was bound to the stake, and Fargo waited as most of the bucks found their way into the other tipis. But at least a dozen settled down on the ground on their blankets, and Fargo waited further till the camp grew silent and dark. A full moon rose to bathe the scene in a pale light, which was a mixed blessing. It let him find his way to Priscilla without groping through moonless blackness but it also exposed him to being spotted by chance.

He rose to his feet, and moving on cautious steps, silent as a panther's prowl, he worked his way around the edges of the camp to the other side. Priscilla had closed her eyes and rested against the stake, and Fargo crept closer, dropped onto his stomach as a Shoshoni emerged from the tipi, and stood before her. Priscilla snapped awake at once and the Shoshoni, wearing only a breechclout, took a piece of fabric from his hand. With a quick motion he tied it around Priscilla's mouth where it hung down beyond her chin, obviously torn from someone's skirt. A second Shoshoni stepped from the tipi and took Priscilla's arms from the stake, but kept her wrists bound together. Both men lifted her and began to drag her to the tipi. Fargo cursed silently. His plans were shattered, along with time.

He reached down to his ankle holster and drew out the double-edged throwing knife. The two Shoshoni had passed in front of him when he rose, measured distance, and flung the knife, an underhanded motion. He was already racing forward, drawing the Colt, as the thin blade hurtled into the back of one Shoshoni's neck, imbedding itself to the hilt. The Indian went down instantly, falling forward, hands clutching at his neck in a last futile gesture. The second Shoshoni halted and stared down at his companion in surprise. Perhaps three or four seconds passed while he saw the hilt of the blade, and surprise translated itself into comprehension.

But Fargo had counted on those precious seconds, and as the Indian's mouth opened to shout, the Colt smashed down on his head. The Shoshoni crumpled to the ground and lay still. Priscilla fell against him, her eyes filled with grateful surprise, and he took the piece of cloth from her lips and motioned for her to be silent. She stayed against him for another long moment, and then he stepped back, took the knife from the Shoshoni's neck, and cut her wrist bonds free. Wiping the knife dry on the Indian's breechclout, he dragged the man to the edge of the trees and did the same with the second one. The Indian would remain unconscious for another ten minutes, Fargo estimated, plenty of time for them to be deep into the forest. But Priscilla pulled back as they started through the trees. "Minnie," she whispered.

"No," Fargo said softly.

"You're going to leave her?" Priscilla frowned.

He nodded, his jaw tight. "She got a lot of people killed, including her own parents. I don't give a damn about her, but that's not the reason I won't get her out. If I try to take her, it'll mean the end for both of us. She won't come quietly. Minnie Thiemann doesn't want to be saved. For better or for worse she wants to stay, to be a Shoshoni. Maybe she'll find whatever she didn't have up to now." Priscilla was silent as he took her hand and led her through the trees to where the Ovaro waited. She climbed onto the saddle in front of him, and he sent the horse moving through the woods at a fast walk.

"Will they come after us?" she asked.

"They'll give a try, but they may give up quickly. The Shoshoni are a practical people. They won't waste time or lives chasing down something that doesn't matter all that much," he said, then put the horse into a trot and began to retrace steps.

The moon had passed the midnight sky when he drew to a halt and slid from the saddle. "We'll rest some. We can't find what we have to find until daylight," he said and set down his bedroll.

"You mean the next instructions," she said, and he nodded. "I'm wondering if it's worth going on," Priscilla said. "There were fourteen of us that started, and they're most all dead now. Seems he gave us more of a chance to get killed than to find the gold."

Fargo's lips pursed. She had given voice to thoughts that pushed at him. Tom Sprague had wanted them to fight to get the gold. *They'll have to work for it,* he had said in one of his early notes. Had he gone too far? Had he been too clever? Had he set traps beyond their ability to survive? Whether he had simply been too Machiavellian, the end result was not a test but a gauntlet of death. Fargo held Priscilla as she settled herself against him.

"It's worth going on. It'll all be yours," he said. "Besides, I don't like the way this has turned out. I'm going to see it through for you." Her lips came against his, sweetness replacing passion before she went to sleep. He lay awake and realized he had come to dislike Tom Sprague for his ruthless cleverness. He went to sleep still carrying the thought, waking when dawn filtered through the tree cover. Priscilla rode the saddle in front of him as he retraced steps again and finally came in sight of the cottonwoods. It was pure good luck that they came upon Priscilla's horse, and she uttered a cry of delight.

"I want to change. Do we have time?" she asked, and Fargo listened to the forest at his back.

"Go on, but hurry," he said, and she slid from the saddle and hurried over to the horse. Stripping off clothes, she pulled a fresh blouse and skirt from one of the saddlebags, and he watched the high-busted beauty of her as she changed clothes. He swung the Ovaro beside her when she finished and knew she saw the ruefulness that touched his face.

"Sorry we didn't have more time?" she asked slyly.

"You know it," he said, and she rode beside him into the cottonwoods. He kept a steady path west as the cottonwoods went on for at least two miles more, and then he saw the trees begin to thin out. The daylight of open land sifted through the trees toward him, and he sent the Ovaro out of the forest. He scanned the edge of the cottonwoods, then moved north along the tree line and suddenly saw the two big trees that had grown together, trunks and branches interlocked. He dismounted and strode to the two trees and spied the mark at once, an *X* painted in black where the two trunks converged. He climbed past the strange formation and, as the note had promised, found the hollow just behind the trunks. Climbing farther, he reached into the hollow and instantly found the roll of paper that filled most of the space.

He drew it out, climbed back from the trunks, and Priscilla was beside him, excitement coloring her face as she read the note with him:

> I confess I am curious as to how many of you are here to find this last note. My admiration for you, and for Fargo, for having come this far. Your prize waits for you. Keep going west. When you come in sight of the Sapphire Mountains, you must look for a small stream that is called Lost Creek. Follow Lost Creek a mile or so north and you'll come to a line cabin that has a chimney of red granite stone.
>
> Under the floorboards you'll find your reward. If no one survives to read this last note, we will all have learned what Bayard Taylor wrote . . . "the leaves of the Judgment Book unfold."
>
> Tom Sprague

Fargo frowned at the note. It was very different from any of the others, simple directions with no passages of scholarly dissertation. But the last lines still offered a cryptic philosophy. He pushed the note into his pocket and started toward the pinto when the sound came to him, horses moving quickly through the trees. The sound grew louder quickly, and Priscilla turned to him, alarm leaping into her eyes. "It seems they're not as practical as you thought," she said.

"Goddamn," he swore. "Hightailing it will get us into a race we might lose." Her eyes questioned, and he pulled the Henry from its saddlecase and handed the rifle to her. "Climb up into the double tree. I'm going to face off with their chief. You draw a bead on him and keep him covered. Don't fire unless I tell you to," he said and helped her climb into the tree. She had positioned herself in a crook between the two trunks when the horsemen rode into sight, the man wearing the buckskin shirt leading eight others.

He rode to a halt and peered at Fargo with a mixture of surprise and uncertainty. Confident that he knew enough Shoshonean to communicate, Fargo forced himself to wait with outward calm even as he felt his palms perspiring. "Where is the woman?" the buckskin shirt asked.

"She is not yours," Fargo said. "You stole her."

"You should have kept running," the Indian said, contempt in his voice.

"You should have given up."

"Where is the woman?" the Shoshoni asked again.

"She is not yours," Fargo repeated.

The Indian raised the carbine. "You are a dead man," he said.

"So are you," Fargo answered.

The buckskin shirt frowned impatiently. "I cannot miss," he said.

"The rifle aimed at you cannot miss," Fargo said, and the Indian's eyes darted to the trees behind him, alarmed surprise flashing in their black orbs. He did not spot Priscilla up in the trees, but Fargo saw him lower the carbine as he decided his foe was not bluffing. Fargo let a moment of satisfaction stab at him. It was going as he had planned. The Shoshoni plainly didn't relish risking a bullet in his chest, yet he had to find a way to save face, not to back down. He had only one way to do it, Fargo knew, and he waited, unmoving, letting the Indian make the decision.

"You . . . me," the Shoshoni said. "We will see if you have courage and honor."

Fargo kept the sigh of relief to himself. He had won the first step. He had turned a pursuit they most likely would have lost into a one-on-one challenge. Now he had to win the second step or it would have all been for nothing. "The woman. I want to see she is here," the Shoshoni said. Fargo swore under his breath and knew he had no choice but to comply. He looked up into the tree and saw the Indian follow his glance. "Tell her to put down the gun," the Shoshoni said.

"Tell your braves to put down their bows," Fargo countered. The buckskin shirt nodded to his men, and they lay their bows on the ground. Fargo motioned to Priscilla. "Come down and put the rifle down," he said. His eyes stayed on the Shoshoni as Priscilla climbed from the tree. When she reached the ground, the Indian stepped forward, reached inside his shirt, and took out a jagged-edged stripping knife. He held it up and then threw it on the ground. Fargo nodded, unholstered the Colt, and dropped it on the ground. The Shoshoni began to circle and Fargo stepped forward to meet his opening moves. The Indian feinted, using his feet and his body, and Fargo let him come in closer and lashed out with a left hook.

The Indian moved quickly, avoiding the blow and diving under it. Fargo tried to twist away, but the man's arms caught him around the legs, and he felt himself go down. As he fell, he managed to bring a chopping right down on the back of the Shoshoni's neck, and the Indian grunted in pain. His grip loosened for an instant, and Fargo kicked his legs free, tried to whirl around, only to feel his foe's hands grasp him by one leg and twist. To avoid a pulled muscle, he didn't resist. Instead, he let himself go with the man's twist as he kicked out with his free leg and felt the kick land on the Indian's chest.

The buckskin shirt grunted, his grip loosened, and again Fargo pulled away. This time he whirled onto his back and saw the Shoshoni dive at him. Lifting both legs, he kicked out and the Indian tried to twist his body sideways. But his momentum was too great, and Fargo's two feet hit into his lower chest. With a gasp of pain he fell, rolled, and Fargo was on his feet, charging at the Shoshoni, who had rolled to one knee. He lifted a left hook, and only the Indian's quickness let him avoid taking the blow squarely. As it was, Fargo's fist landed alongside his jaw and sent him flying backward. Fargo charged again as the Shoshoni rolled, rolled again, and he saw the Indian's arm come up, his hand raised, clasped around a rock.

Fargo tried to duck, but the rock was already hurtling at him. It struck him alongside the temple, and he went down, flashing colors exploding in his head. The Shoshoni barreled into him, and Fargo's head hit against the ground. Strangely enough, the blow cleared away the flashing colors, but the Indian's hands were already around his throat. Using all the strength of his leg muscles, Fargo managed to bring up one leg, pushed, and the man half rolled to one side. But he had his own, wiry strength, and he kept his grip until Fargo brought up a looping right that smashed into the side of his face. He uttered a

Shoshoni curse as he fell away, and Fargo whirled from his grasp.

Fargo pushed to his feet, his head cleared but his temple throbbing. The Shoshoni came at him again, feinting to the left, then to the right, then darting forward in a crouch. Fargo shot out a straight left that caught the Indian on the jaw and stopped his forward motion. A right that followed caught him alongside the jaw and sent him staggering backward. Fargo stepped in, too quickly, too eagerly, and saw his whistling left hook hit only air as the buckskin shirt dropped below it. Flinging his body sideways, the Shoshoni crashed into his foe's ankles, and Fargo found himself toppling forward as his feet were swept out from under him. Striking upward, the Indian drove a blow into his opponent's stomach, and Fargo grunted as the air was driven from him. He flung himself forward, the Indian's next blow landing against his hip, rolled, and had regained one knee as the figure charged at him.

Swinging a left hook from one knee, bringing it up and around with all his strength, he caught the charging figure flush on the jaw. The buckskin shirt halted, staggered, and Fargo's right sent him sailing, his body arched as if in a backward somersault. He hit the ground, shuddered, and lay still. Fargo rose to his feet and approached the man with caution. But the Shoshoni stayed unmoving. Fargo lifted him by his buckskin shirt and dropped him down again, and the figure groaned and his eyes fluttered. Fargo's gaze went to the Shoshoni who looked on. "Over. Finished," Fargo said and gestured to the buckskin shirt. "Take him."

Wordlessly, two of the braves stepped forward,

lifted their leader, and deposited him onto his horse. Another picked up the jagged stripping knife and took it with him. They moved silently away to disappear into the trees, and Fargo sank onto one knee and winced as he drew a deep breath. Priscilla came to him, cradled his head against her breasts and he enjoyed the soft warmth of her. He rose, finally, picked up the Colt, and holstered it. "It's all over now?" Priscilla asked.

"Probably," Fargo said, and she gave him a sidelong glance.

"That's hardly reassuring," she said.

"I didn't kill him," Fargo said.

"Meaning he'll try again?"

"Some tribes have different codes of honor from others," Fargo began to explain when the high-pitched cry split the air, followed by the sound of galloping hooves. Fargo pushed Priscilla aside as he whirled and drew the Colt, the whooping cry reverberating through the trees again. The pony burst from the trees, charging at him, the Shoshoni atop the steed, brandishing the carbine. Fargo waited before he raised the Colt and fired a single shot, and the buckskin shirt tore apart in a shower of red. The figure flew sideways from the pony and lay still once and for all.

Priscilla stared down at the Indian, shock in her eyes. "I don't understand. He ran right at you, but he was waving the rifle," she said.

"It was the code. When I won and didn't kill him, I dishonored him. I hoped he wasn't part of that code but he was," Fargo said. "He attacked to be killed and his honor restored."

Priscilla turned away. "Take me out of here," she said and pulled herself onto her horse. He swung onto the Ovaro and rode on with her as the line of braves moved slowly through the trees. She rode almost a half hour beside him before she spoke again. "How much longer before we reach where we're going?" she asked.

"You rushing to or away?" he questioned.

"Both," she said. "I want this over. I want to go back, to get away from things I don't understand. The only good that's come out of this is you."

"We ought to see the Sapphire Mountains in another day or two," he told her, and, satisfied, she rode on in silence again. He held a steady pace, and Priscilla continued to ride immersed in her own thoughts. When night came and he found a hollow of aspen in which to bed down, she made love to him with a newfound desperation, as though she were trying to let the body wash away the mind. Exploration, discovery, desire—they all were clothed in a new dimension that made them more intense, and she clung to him with every part of her body. Finally, when her screams died away, she slept tight against him as though even in sleep she seethed.

But when morning came, she had regained her old self, and he knew she had, for a while, at least, come to terms with the pain and hurt she could understand and the concepts she couldn't. The terrain allowed them to make good time, and when the day drew to an end, the distant peaks of the Sapphire Mountains were visible. Fargo made camp beside a stream, and Priscilla's lovemaking made the night pass quickly. The desperation had left, and she reveled once again in the simple pleasures of discovery and exploration. She urged him to savor every part of her with hands, lips, tongue, and she did the same to him. When her final throbbing contractions grew still, she lay breathlessly against him until she found her voice.

"Ice cream," she murmured, and he frowned at her. "I understand about liking ice cream. I really understand now," she explained. "I understand so much I never did before, and yet there's so much I don't understand."

"It takes time and it's hardly ever easy," he told her. She murmured and fell asleep in his arms. He was glad the end was near, he realized. It had been a strange odyssey, planned with ruthless cleverness and directed from beyond the grave. As he closed his eyes, he wondered if the real truth about Tom Sprague would ever be known. He pushed aside his thoughts and slept until the morning dawned with a hot sun. When Priscilla rose and was ready to ride, he kept the horses at a walk through low land where the cool of the night still clung to the earth.

He was more than happy when they came onto a bearded old man with a wrinkled face and sharp blue eyes camped beside a mule and a leather bag of tools. " 'Morning, friend," Fargo offered. "You passing through or do you know this territory?"

"Been passing through for twenty years," the old man said wryly.

Fargo smiled. "You a tinker?"

"The best," the old man said.

"I'm looking for a place. They call it Lost Creek," Fargo said.

"Kind of fits," the man said.

"What fits?" Fargo asked.

"You're lost and you're looking for Lost Creek," he said.

"You've a sense of humor, friend. Is that all you have?"

"Head south. It'll take looking for. They named it well," the man said. "Look for a small draw, lots of sage in bloom. That's the best I can do."

"Much obliged," Fargo said and turned the pinto south. He rode slowly, Priscilla beside him, and they had gone some five miles when he spied the shallow draw and in the center of it, the small creek. He followed it as it wandered, staying in the draw, and his eyes surveyed the low ridge. He led the way past two ramshackle huts and a house that had fallen in on itself. When a cabin came into sight, he slowed but the chimney was fashioned of gray and white stone so he rode on. The creek left the draw when the table of land changed and made its way across a low plateau well covered with serviceberry. The noon sun was high and hot when Fargo saw another cabin, set back a few hundred yards from the creek, and he heard Priscilla's short gasp as a chimney of red granite stones rose over the roof.

"That's got to be it," she murmured as he rode toward the cabin, halted outside the closed door, and swung to the ground. Priscilla was beside him as he knocked, waited, and when no one answered, he turned the doorknob. The door swung open, and he entered to see a single room, sparsely furnished with two wicker chairs and a sagging dresser against one wall. Fargo's eyes went to the floorboards, hand-hewn, wide lengths of pine. He knelt down, found he couldn't wedge his fingers between the floorboards, and hurried outside to the Ovaro where he fetched a short-handled spade from his saddlebag.

The floorboards lifted as he used the spade, and

Priscilla dropped to her knees beside him as he took up the first one, then the next, and when he lifted the third one, she gave a sharp, gasped cry as she spied the long, iron strongbox in a hollowed-out section of earth. Fargo reached down and lifted the strongbox, then frowned. It was lighter than he'd expected, and his fingers went to the simple, unlocked latch and pulled it open. He lifted the lid and stared inside. This time Priscilla's sharp gasp was not one of excitement but one of shock and dismay. The strongbox was empty, except for one gold coin.

9

Fargo's glance went to Priscilla, and he saw the shock in her face turn into shattering disappointment. "It's been stolen. The gold's been stolen," she said.

Fargo's eyes returned to the single gold coin inside the strongbox. He stared at it, transfixed for what seemed an endless minute. But he felt his own initial surprise slowly taking on another shape as thoughts whirled through his head, tumbling, twisting, shooting off in all directions as though they were so many horses on a carousel gone awry. But they stopped spinning and took shape, and suddenly the last lines in Tom Sprague's last note had a new clarity.

Suddenly so many things were falling into place, the single gold coin the final, mocking taunt. "No, it wasn't stolen," he said, and Priscilla frowned at him with uncomprehending disbelief.

"Of course it was stolen. It's gone, isn't it?" she returned.

"No, it's not gone. That's all there ever was. That's your gold fortune," Fargo said, and Priscilla's mouth fell open.

"No, you're mistaken. What makes you even think that?" she said.

"A thief would have taken everything. A thief

wouldn't have left a single gold coin," Fargo said. "That gold coin is a statement, a last laugh. It explains so many other things."

"Such as?"

"Everything that's happened. The gold fortune was never a challenge for you to win. It was a carrot dangled in front of your noses, everything planned to kill as many of you as possible." He paused at the shattered shock in her face and felt awed by the diabolic cleverness of Tom Sprague. "It was also planned to make it all seem to be the result of bad luck, accidents, fate. He planned it all so he couldn't be accused of anything."

"But why?" Priscilla threw at him.

Fargo frowned. "I don't know the answer to that. I might know if the others had been more honest with me. But they weren't."

"I can't believe this," Priscilla muttered.

"It makes everything fit. He tricked you and enjoyed every minute of it. He used human nature and greed and brought you along step by step. You were right when you said it seemed he was giving you more chance to get killed than to find the gold. That's exactly the way he planned it."

Priscilla's face stayed wreathed in shock. "He succeeded, didn't he? Almost everybody's been killed," she said. "It came out the way he expected it would."

"Pretty much so," Fargo agreed. "Though he couldn't be sure. His last note said he was curious how many made it here."

"The morbid bastard," Priscilla said bitterly.

Fargo frowned as he reached into his pocket and brought out the last note. He reread the last paragraph aloud.

"If no one survives to read this last note, we will all have learned what Bayard Taylor wrote . . . *the leaves of the Judgment Book unfold.*" The reference to the Judgement Book held the key. Their deaths had been a judgement, one that he had arranged. Vengeance, revenge—they were the motivating force. But there was more, hidden in the last sentences. *If no one survives . . . we will all have learned. . . . the leaves of the Judgement Book unfold.* They would *all* have learned the lesson, by their deaths, by being unable to be here. But Tom Sprague had finally made a mistake. He had stumbled over his own cleverness. *We will all have learned,* Fargo read again. Not just those who didn't make it, not just those who, by their absence, signaled their fate in that Judgement Book. Fargo uttered a wry snort and drew a quick frown from Priscilla.

"He's not dead," Fargo said.

"What are you talking about?" she asked.

"Tom Sprague. He's alive."

"You mean his legacy still lives."

"No, I mean he's alive," Fargo said.

"That's ridiculous."

"Yes, but it's so."

"You saw the death certificate from the doctor in Rockville and the burial deed from the undertaker," Priscilla reminded him.

"I know, but I also know that a man clever enough to plan everything he did is clever enough to have arranged that. I'm telling you he's alive. That's the last piece that makes everything fit. He didn't plan it all to lie in his grave, not knowing the results. He planned it so he could enjoy the final results, so he could have that final laugh. Revenge doesn't mean much if you can't enjoy it," Fargo said and pushed to his feet.

"Where are you going?" Priscilla asked as he started for the door.

"To check out what I've just said," he tossed back and heard her hurry to rise and scramble after him. He was outside, kneeling down alongside the bushes near the side of the cabin when she arrived. He pointed to the tracks in the ground, footprints that led along the side of the cabin to the door, others that led away from the house. The tracks overlapped each other, and Fargo counted at least ten trails. He knelt down, and his fingers moved along the line of footprints nearest him. "Not more than a few days old," he said.

"Meaning what?"

"Meaning somebody has made steady, numerous trips to the cabin," Fargo said. "The last one only a few days ago."

"Tom Sprague? You really think that?" Priscilla questioned.

"I'd bet on it. I aim to find out," Fargo said.

"How?" she asked, and he rose and followed the tracks to where they went into the serviceberry and a carpet of leaves quickly erased the trail. "I could try and pick up more tracks farther on, but I've a better way," he said, and Priscilla's eyes questioned. "You lose the fox's trail, you let the fox come back to the henhouse," he said, then took her arm and led her into the serviceberry that afforded a thick, shrubby cover and let them see the cabin. He retrieved the horses and tethered them a hundred yards deeper into the trees. Settling down beside her, he felt an excitement pulling at him. Tom Sprague had ceased to be a series of letters, a voice from the grave. He was real, flesh and blood alive, Fargo was certain, and he stretched out in the grass.

Priscilla lay down beside him, and the sun began to lower to finally vanish over the horizon. "How long do we wait?" Priscilla asked.

"The freshest prints were only a few days old. I'd say he visits every three or four days," Fargo said. "Or nights."

"We just stay here and wait."

"And be quiet," he said.

"I still can't believe any of it," she said, but she fell silent and stayed that way as the night grew deep and soon he heard her steady breathing as she fell asleep. He slept in small spurts, never more than half-asleep at any time, but the night stayed silent, and he was awake with the morning sun as Priscilla stirred and sat up.

"I don't expect he'll come at this hour. Go back to the creek and freshen up. I'll wait here," he said, and she hurried away to return looking scrubbed and grave-faced. He went to the creek then, and she was munching on a small bush of wild cherries when he returned.

"What if he doesn't come?" she asked.

"He will. Somebody's been making regular visits."

"Maybe somebody who used the cabin," she said.

He peered at her. "You don't want to believe he's alive, do you?" Fargo said.

"No," she said, her voice barely audible.

"Why not?"

"It'd be too much. I'll accept that it was all planned, carefully and cleverly planned, but I don't want to face him. I'd rather just leave and be grateful I'm alive," she said.

"I don't like being played for a fool. I don't like my neck put on the line. I could have been killed along with the others. I'm going to see that he pays for it," Fargo said, and Priscilla looked unhappy as she sat down beside him. The morning began to lengthen when suddenly Fargo's wild-creature hearing caught the sound of movement in the trees behind the cabin. He rose to one knee at once and peered through the shrubby serviceberry to see a figure emerge from the bushes and carefully edge to the open cabin door. He saw a tall man, well-built, wearing his age with muscled grace, graying hair, and a sharp, tight-skinned face. He had a sling of prospector's tools over one shoulder, and he paused for a moment at the cabin door before entering.

Fargo was moving forward in a fast lope at once, and he reached the doorway to see the figure staring down at the floorboards that had been pulled up and the empty strongbox. The man heard him as he entered, and turned, a tiny furrow on his brow, but his face expressionless. "Hello," he said, a good, resonant voice. "Sorry to barge in. This your place?"

"No. Is it yours?" Fargo asked.

The man offered a polite smile as he shrugged, and Fargo saw his eyes go to Priscilla as she appeared. "I've used it once or twice," he said. His eyes went to the floorboards. "Looks as though somebody else has been here."

"So it does. My name's Fargo, Skye Fargo, and this is Priscilla Dale," Fargo introduced.

"Sam Keenan," the man said.

Fargo's glance went to the tools in the canvas sling. "Prospector?" he asked.

"That's right," the man said, and Fargo kept a grim

smile to himself. The man was cool, a bland expression on his face. But Fargo had seen his eyes narrow for just an instant when he'd introduced himself and Priscilla. "You two alone?" the man asked.

Fargo's smile stayed within, but the grimness turned to triumph. He had the answer he wanted. "Yep, just the two of us," he said. "You're a long way from prospecting country. You get yourself lost?"

"Inadvertently." The man smiled.

This time Fargo's smile was open, pleasant, almost chiding. "You know, I've talked with prospectors all over the country—old men, middle-aged men, young hopefuls. I've drunk with them, eaten with them, played poker with them. And you know, in all those times and over all those years, I've never heard one of them ever use the word *inadvertently,*" Fargo said, and the smile left his face. "That's no prospector's word. That's a schoolteacher's word, and you're Tom Sprague, you clever bastard."

The man's eyes narrowed and grew hard, but he didn't shout denials. He let his eyes go to Priscilla as he studied her. "I never invited a Priscilla Dale," he said.

"You invited my mother, Harriet Dale," Priscilla said.

Tom Sprague brought his eyes back to Fargo. "How did you know?" he asked.

"Your last note. You got clever once too often," Fargo said. "Why'd you do it? Revenge for what?"

"Revenge for all the times every one of them refused to help me. They were all glad to take from me, but none of them was ever willing to help me when I wanted help. Byron had plenty of money then. He was on a winning streak, and I offered him a good, fair business proposition. He turned me down, laughed at me. Then there were the Forstmanns and Jake and Sarah Dowd. They borrowed money from me, but never paid me back. Sam and Nedda Grafton asked to stay at my place. They agreed to pay rent and money for board. They never did and ran off in the night, owing me six months' rent."

"Donna?" Fargo queried.

"That two-timing, unfaithful woman. I used to see her with other men. She'd always have some terrible excuse about my being away teaching at boarding schools."

"So you had a grudge against each and every one of them."

"They were all rotten," the man said.

"What did you have against my mother?" Priscilla cut in.

"After your father died, she let me think she might marry me. I gave her money to help her out, paid off a loan for her, and then she threw me over," Tom Sprague shot back.

"So you figured out a way to kill off all of them," Fargo said.

"I gave them a chance," Tom Sprague said.

"Hell, you did. You set them up to be killed. Me, too," Fargo said. "You're a murderer, a very clever one but a murderer," Fargo said.

Tom Sprague's smile was deprecatory. "That is something you can never prove. They were all killed by natural disasters, poor judgement, Shoshoni attacks, unforseen accidents. You can never prove I murderered a single one of them."

Fargo's hand rested on the butt of the Colt. "I'm taking you back," he said.

Tom Sprague shrugged. "I don't mind. I intended to go back anyway. But you're wasting your time. I never touched a one of them. You can't accuse a man of murdering someone he's never touched. You're just indulging in your own frustrations, Fargo."

"You're going back," Fargo said doggedly.

"Indulge yourself. No sheriff will jail me. No judge will convict me," Tom Sprague said. His unconcern was not an act, Fargo knew, and he swore silently.

"You've a horse somewhere?" he inquired.

"A half mile down the creek," Sprague said.

"Start walking," Fargo grunted and drew his Colt. Sprague gave him a chiding smile as he began to walk. Priscilla brought her horse and the Ovaro, and Fargo followed Sprague to a tent where a short-legged roan waited. After he gathered his things, Fargo tied his hands loosely enough for him to grasp the saddle horn. "Ride in front of me. You know the way back," Fargo said as they started east. He dropped back a half dozen feet, and Priscilla swung in beside him, her voice low.

"You know he's right," she said. "Why are you taking him back?"

"To hang for murder."

"But he never touched a one of them. He was too clever. You said so yourself," Priscilla countered. "I hate his getting away scot-free as much as you do, but you know that's what will happen."

"He's going back," Fargo repeated, his voice cold steel.

Priscilla gave a tiny half shrug. "I'd rather spend the time putting it all behind us, just the two of us."

"We'll get to that later," Fargo said, and she looked at him with a combination of helplessness and reproach. He said nothing more, and she rode quietly beside him. Fargo allowed Sprague to be untied when they camped for supper, but tied him again when the meal was finished.

"Come now, Fargo. I'm hardly the desperate prisoner," the man said affably.

"Not yet but you will be," Fargo answered. "The closer a man gets to hanging, the more desperate he becomes."

Sprague laughed. "But I'm not getting any closer to hanging. How long are you going to keep up this farce, my friend?"

"Long enough to see you convicted," Fargo said and lay down on his bedroll. Priscilla came to sleep alongside him, and he was aware of the questioning glances she tossed at him. But he remained adamant as the days went by. They had camped only a day's ride from Rockville when Tom Sprague rested his bound hands on his knees.

"I must say I'm disappointed in you, Fargo," he said. "I expected you to be more of a realist. Even the lovely young lady can't understand all this childish stubbornness. I've seen it in her eyes."

"Me, too," Fargo said.

"Yet you persist, knowing the sheriff will turn me loose at once. Amazing," the man said.

"Humor me, cousin," Fargo said coldly.

"Why not? In fact, I've become quite curious how you intend to accuse me of murder. It should really be amusing," Tom Sprague said.

"I figure to enjoy it," Fargo growled. "You see, I'm betting that the man they buried as you has at least one bullet hole in him." Tom Sprague's eyes narrowed, and his cool confidence suddenly vanished as the corners of his mouth twitched. "I'll have the body dug up if I have to," Fargo went on. "Then I'll show him your note lying to me about the doctors saying you were going to die from a long illness. When I'm finished, it's going to be damn clear that you shot the man they buried so you'd be able to switch identities with him." He paused and saw cold anger forming in Tom Sprague's eyes. "And you know what, my scholarly friend, he's going to be the murder they'll hang you for. You were right about the others. You can't be accused of murdering someone you never touched. We'll make do with the one you did touch. So far as the hangman's noose is concerned, one's as good as twelve."

Tom Sprague's lips pursed. "I'm glad to see that my first estimate of you was correct," he said, a slow smile returning to his face. "It's always satisfying to see one's confidence rewarded."

"You'll excuse me if I don't say thanks," Fargo returned. "Now let's move. We've some distance to cover."

"And I've been riding for days in this shirt. I'm hot and uncomfortable. May I get a fresh shirt out of my saddlebag?" the man asked. Fargo nodded and untied his hands and slid from the saddle.

"I'll stretch. I'm feeling tired," Priscilla said as she dismounted. Fargo watched Tom Sprague pull a fresh shirt from his saddlebag, take off the old one, and change. The man turned back to his saddlebag to put away his old shirt, and when he turned from the horse, Fargo saw the small pistol in his hand, a Beal's army revolver with the barrel shortened. He only half turned, the gun pointed at Priscilla. "One wrong move and she's dead," the man said. "You see, anybody can underestimate someone."

"So they can," Fargo agreed and cursed inwardly. He had been careless, too anxious to bring in Sprague. He swore at himself again as the man kept the gun trained on Priscilla.

"Drop your gun, Fargo," Sprague said. "Don't underestimate me twice."

"I never did. I just got sloppy," Fargo said.

"Not quite a compliment in return, but it will have to do," the man said. "Now, the gun, please." Fargo lifted the Colt from its holster and let it slide to the ground. "Kick it over here," Sprague ordered, and he obeyed. Fargo then let his muscles tighten. A line of thick sagebrush was but a half dozen feet from him, and he knew Tom Sprague was not about to let him walk away. The man was both ruthless and clever, Fargo reminded himself. He waited as the Colt came to a stop a few inches from Sprague, then held his breath as the man reached down to pick up the gun. The short-barreled revolver turned away from Priscilla for a moment, and Fargo dived, flinging himself sideways into the brush. "Goddamn," Sprague cursed as he straightened up and fired, but Fargo was into the sagebrush already, rolling, turning his body first one way then the other.

The man did not waste another shot. Instead, he reached out, yanked Priscilla toward him, and pulled her up into the saddle in front of him. He sent the horse into an instant gallop and raced away. Fargo pushed himself up from the sagebrush and ran to the Ovaro, leaped onto the horse, and gave chase. But he stayed back, unwilling to give the man a clear shot.

Sprague knew he followed, but he concentrated on steering his horse through a stand of quaking aspen, then into a forest of Rocky Mountain maple. The day slid into dusk, and the dusk into night, and Fargo heard his quarry continuing on as the moon rose to afford a fitful light.

He increased the Ovaro's speed, the night giving Sprague less chance for a clear shot at him. The man was but a few hundred feet ahead of him in the forest, and Fargo spurred the Ovaro on faster, swung out to pass Tom Sprague, then cut in front and pass him again on the other side. He glimpsed the man swiveling his head in one direction then the other, and Fargo came up directly behind him until Sprague turned and fired two shots. Fargo veered away, then came in closer from the left side, and Sprague fired again. Again Fargo peeled away. He raced the Ovaro forward, cut in front of the man once more, and Sprague fired again. Fargo allowed a tight smile to touch his lips. Sprague was becoming increasingly rattled and fired off two more shots from the Colt. But he still had the small revolver.

Fargo made two more passes at the man and heard him fire the last of the Colt's bullets, then switch to the Beal. Circling Sprague in erratic circles, he continued to unnerve the man but, conscious of the few bullets he had left, he had stopped firing wildly. His horse had slowed, carrying two riders, and Fargo, drawing opposite the man, sent the Ovaro directly at the man. Lying almost flat in the saddle as the pinto raced forward, he leaped to the ground as the horse continued on. Fargo hit the ground on the balls of his feet, stumbled, caught himself, and ran forward as he saw Sprague fire at the oncoming Ovaro. The Ovaro veered to the right, and Sprague reined almost to a halt, frowning after the horse.

He whirled in the saddle, but he was hampered by Priscilla's body in front of him, and Fargo was diving upward as he got a wild shot off. Slamming into the man, Fargo carried him to the ground where Sprague landed half on his side. Fargo's roundhouse left caught the man alongside the face, and Sprague rolled, brought up the pistol, but Fargo's following right slammed into his abdomen. Sprague doubled over as he fell backward, and Fargo dived onto him. He grabbed at the man's gun hand, but Sprague twisted away and started to bring the short-barrel pistol around when Fargo shot out a backhanded blow. He felt Sprague's arm go back and up, then the shot exploded, and he saw Tom Sprague's head fly apart.

On one knee Fargo stared at the twisted figure that suddenly looked not unlike a headless doll. He let out a deep breath as he rose to his feet, pulled the Colt from the man's belt, and turned to Priscilla, who had slid from the horse. She came to him and she was trembling. He walked to the Ovaro and lifted her onto the saddle, and she rode back in silence until they came to her horse. "Bullet, noose, I suppose it doesn't make all that much difference," she said.

"Not when it's all said and done," he agreed. "All because he had to have his revenge."

"Proof you can be twisted and clever at the same time," she said. "Take me away someplace, Fargo, to a lost creek of our own. Let me learn again all the things I learned with you before. That'll make up for everything else that's happened."

"Sounds like a damn good idea," he said, and her hand came into his as he turned northward. No revenge at Lost Creek this time. Just pleasure.

1860, Russian America—
The vast and unforgiving land that will become Alaska
where freezing cold makes every moment a hunt
for life or a struggle against death . . .

Pete MacKenzie was right where they said he'd be—
five miles east of the village of Alakanuk, at the bend
of the creek. There the bitter wind howled through the
yellow cedar and picked up blasts of powdery snow
from the surrounding hills. From far off echoed the
call of a lone wolf. From nearby came the gurgle of
water under the first coat of winter ice and the rhyth-
mic squeak of the rawhide thong against the rough
bark of a branch.

Suspended high above the fresh snow, MacKenzie's
frozen corpse swung back and forth in the wind. His
black hair was matted by snow, purplish face swollen
almost beyond recognition. His hands hung heavy by
his sides, the gloved fingers tipped with icicles.

The tall man stood for a long time, taking in the sight as the dim October light faded slowly. His lake blue eyes registered everything—the color of the dead man's flesh, the dark holes where four bullets had pierced the front of the moose-skin jacket, the tracks of frustrated wolves in the snow below. Death had been quick. And then MacKenzie's body had been hauled up high and left as some kind of warning. But what kind of warning?

Fargo swore under his breath. If only he'd got word from Pete sooner. Maybe he could have saved him. He cursed the senseless murder of a man as good as Pete MacKenzie. Cursed whoever did it. Cursed fate for keeping Pete's message from reaching him until it was too late. He glanced about him at the snow-covered creek bank and the dark forest that blanketed the hills to the banks of the Yukon River just a few miles away.

All around, the vast miles of northland seemed to press in on him, and he heard again the call of wolves, the creak of the tall trees as they swayed in the wind. Night was coming on, and winter was on the way—a helluva time to be up in Russian America, the wildest land on earth, a brutal place where only the brutal survived. He'd been up here once, a long time ago when he'd met up with Pete MacKenzie. And now he'd come back to find Pete dead.

Fargo drew his Colt and fired. The shot reverberated, and a ptarmigan scuttled from beneath a nearby thicket. MacKenzie's body dropped onto the soft snow. Fargo drew his knife and cut the rawhide thong into pieces, then walked into the trees, his swallowtail snowshoes leaving a wide track in the fresh powder. He gathered several long branches and bent to the task of fashioning a travois. Fifteen minutes later, with MacKenzie's body strapped to the makeshift carrier, Fargo set off, hiking back toward the tiny fishing village of Alakanuk. Behind him, he dragged the body of Pete MacKenzie.

MacKenzie had been one of the best trackers in the north. A silent man, a steady man, a man who could read the wind and move just as swiftly. He'd been a man who knew the ways of the north—where to set rabbit snares, find caribou herds and salmon. How to trap beaver, leaving the pregnant females so there'd be more the following year. How to keep warm in the blizzard. How to walk carefully, never making the one mistake that this unforgiving land could kill you for.

Pete MacKenzie had made a mistake somewhere along the way. But it wasn't the land that had killed him. Fargo knew he'd have to find whoever did it. It didn't matter that MacKenzie had been dead for at least a week and that the murderer could be hundreds of miles away by now. It didn't matter that winter was about to hit, and the whole territory would soon be a frozen wasteland traveled only by wolves. Nothing mattered except finding the killer.

And as he tramped on through the darkening night, Fargo found himself thinking back to the night he got his last message from Pete MacKenzie . . .

He'd found himself in Vancouver that night, at the Rusty Bullet Saloon with a buxom blonde named Sally on one knee and a straight flush spread out before him, facedown on the table. He was off two hundred dollars, but winning this hand would put him well ahead for the night. He glanced into the cold eyes of the mustachioed gambling man sitting opposite him.

"Your bet, Mr. Fargo," the gambler said with a brief smile, his voice smooth as honey.

Sally flashed Fargo an encouraging smile and fluffed her blond hair. Fargo's eyes narrowed a moment, and he pretended to hesitate. His hand hovered over his remaining pile of silver and greenbacks, and then he bent the edges of the cards upward as if convincing himself to lay a bet. With another glance toward the gambler, Fargo slowly pushed the remainder of his pile of silver and bills to the center of the table.

"Wow," Sally said. She started to lean over to kiss him, but Fargo held her off, concentrating. She pouted. The men crowding around the table murmured, and Fargo stroked his chin as if reconsidering, too late, what he'd done. His opponent's face was made of stone, but Fargo saw the secret smile behind the ice-cold eyes. The gambler brought his manicured hand confidently toward his tall pile of coins. The fingers touched the pile, then Fargo saw the hand hesitate as the gambler's eyes glanced up, flickered, and went cold. He suddenly snapped his cards together with a smart click.

"You win," he said to Fargo.

The crowd muttered in disappointment as Fargo took back his pile of money.

"I saw that," a voice said, cutting through the hubbub. "I saw that, little lady." Sally gave a jump, then laughed as if she had accidentally slipped off Fargo's knee. She readjusted herself with a flutter of red silk and lace.

The gambler hastily swept up his money and was starting to rise from the table when a short wiry man with a mop of frizzy silver hair and a long beard pushed his way to the front and grabbed one of the gambler's lapels.

In that instant, Sally laughed again nervously and pulled Fargo's hand from her waist upward to cover the soft, full mound of her breast.

"Want to go upstairs now, big man?" she breathed into his ear.

But Fargo pushed her away and slowly stood as he watched the gambler trying to shake off the little man who had a firm grip on his gleaming white jacket.

"I saw that pretty yellow chicken give you the signal!" the old man shouted at the gambler. "I saw those big eyes blinking at you and don't you deny it!"

Sally's wide blue eyes met Fargo's, and he saw the terror in them. She shook her head and then tried a smile on him, but it was guilty as all hell. The crowd was pressing in on them, deadly silent, hanging on every word of the drama. Several of the burly men listening had their hands on their pistols.

"Ridiculous!" the gambler protested. "I deny it, old man. You're seeing things."

Sally was trying to slip away, but Fargo reached out and jerked her towards him, then held her pinioned against him. "What do you say?" he said low in her ear. Sally shook her head violently, struggling in his powerful hold. He gripped her a little harder.

"Let go of her!" the gambler suddenly shouted, his face livid.

"I told you it wouldn't work," Sally suddenly shrieked at him, sobs in her voice. "I told you we wouldn't get away with it!"

At this the men surrounding the table burst into an uproar. Before Fargo could take a step forward, hands pulled the gambler into the crowd and the contents of his pockets were emptied onto the table. The gambler shouted and struggled, but the men hoisted him over their heads and passed him, hand to hand, toward the door.

"Get out," Fargo said quietly to the blond woman cowering beside him. Sally spun about and disappeared into the crowd. A loud laugh came from the other end of the room where, Fargo guessed, the rambunctious crowd had tossed the gambler out the batwing doors and into the muddy street. The gambler's coins and greenbacks were piled on the center of the table.

"Drinks are on me!" Fargo shouted.

The Rusty Bullet crowd roared its approval. Fargo motioned toward the gray-haired man to join him, and they sat down at the table as the noise gradually subsided.

Fargo eyed the old man before him. A trapper or a prospector maybe. His bright blue eyes were set deep in a face lined with hard living and burned dark by the sun. His hands were as knobby as old apple trees, and several fingers were missing their last joints. Bad frostbite, Fargo guessed.

"Name's Skye Fargo," he said. "Much obliged to

you." Fargo pushed half the pile of money toward the old man, who eyed it, halved it again, pocketed the smaller pile and pushed the rest back toward Fargo.

"I only take fair pay, what's coming to me," the old man explained. "I've heard of you. My name's Sixty." They shook hands and Fargo ordered a round of beers.

"What kind of name's that?" Fargo asked.

"Sixty-Mile Sam," he answered. "That's my full name. I used to be real good with a dog sled. Took a trip up the Yukon once and made sixty miles a day for nigh on fifteen days." The old man paused a moment, then shook off the memory. "Nobody'd ever done that before. Not since, neither!"

The beers arrived and they raised their mugs, clacked them, and drank down.

"What're you doing so far south?" Fargo asked.

Sixty looked wistful for a moment.

"My brother got sick a few years back so I went on down to Minnesota to visit him. God, it's hot down there. Well, he didn't get better and I stayed with him. Last month he died." Sixty paused and wiped his mouth on his sleeve. His eyes sought Fargo's. "I've been hanging around here trying to think where to go next." He paused again as if remembering something far away. "But that land up there's damn hard on a man," he said softly. "And I'm getting old."

Fargo started to answer when he became aware of a tall man who had come to stand over their table. He glanced up and recognized a face he'd noticed earlier in the crowd, watching the card game. The stranger was powerfully built with a deep chest and long limbs. His brown hair was thick and waved back from a tall square forehead. Two piercing brown eyes looked at him from beneath thick black brows. He wore a dress jacket and a vest with a subtle brocade pattern, a high white collar, and no stickpin. Fargo pegged him for a foreigner.

"Excuse me," the gentleman said in a heavy accent. "I've been told that you are Mr. Skye Fargo, the famous Trailsman." Fargo nodded. "May I sit down please to discuss some business?" Fargo indicated a chair and cleared the table of the remaining money as the foreigner seated himself.

"Please allow me to introduce myself," he said. "I am Count Vasili Victoroff. From the Ukraine."

"And this is Sixty-Mile Sam," Fargo put in. The count hardly glanced toward the old man, but kept his dark eyes trained on Fargo.

"I have heard you are a remarkable man," Victoroff said. "I have heard you can find trails where no one else can, that you can track down anyone, find anything in the wilderness."

"You bet he can," Sixty put in. "Heard tell he's the best in the business."

"What's the job?" Fargo asked. Count Victoroff laughed heartily.

"*Da, da.* That is what I like so much about you Americans," he said, chuckling. "Always to the point. Now, in Russia, we would take our time. Have some vodka, talk about anything but business." Fargo gestured to the bartender to bring another drink. The count, seeing his gesture, chuckled again.

"So," Fargo said.

"So," the count said slowly, his eyes searching

Fargo's face for a long moment. "It's about . . . my daughter." The beer arrived, and the count looked at it distastefully, then took a tentative sip. Fargo watched him closely. "Yes, my daughter, Natasha. You see, she was taken from me, kidnapped."

Fargo didn't answer, but sat listening and watching the Russian count. When Fargo didn't speak, the count continued. "Well, actually she is not my daughter. She is my ward and I am her guardian. It is the same thing in my country." Sixty caught Fargo's eye and grinned. The count took another sip of the beer.

"How long's she been gone?"

"Six months," the count said. "And I've been looking for them, for her, ever since."

"And you know who took her?"

"Da! Da!" the count's voice rose with suppressed rage. "She was taken right from my villa at my estate! Right out from under my nose by a band of local thugs. Criminal elements of the worst kind." The count paused, his face reddened, and he hit the table with his fist. "It was . . . unbelievable!"

"And you've tracked them to America," Fargo said.

"You are a smart man," the count said. "I have found these thieves. *Da,* I have found out where they are hiding with my Natasha. They have a camp far up in the wilderness, in the Russian colony up north. I found out where. Almost where. Now I need someone very good. I am sure you are just the one."

"Sorry," Fargo said. He took a slow swallow of beer and put the mug down on the table, catching the surprised glance from Sixty, who had been closely following the conversation. "Sorry, I'm not your man."

The count sat back in his chair and regarded Fargo for a long moment.

"May I ask why?"

"I have my reasons," Fargo said shortly. The one reason was simple. He had a gut feeling about Count Victoroff. And his gut feeling told him that something about the story wasn't true. And if a man was going to lie to you from the very beginning, he'd be lying to you clear to the end. Fargo thought about the girl, Natasha, for a moment and wondered if she even existed. The tale sounded too incredible to believe. A band of Russian bandits kidnapped a girl and took her halfway around the world?

"Oh, I see the problem," the count said smoothly. He fished around in his coat pocket for a moment and pulled out a very large coin purse. He laid it quietly on the table between them. Fargo didn't even look at it, but just shook his head. The count opened the bag and dumped the coins on the table. Fine gold glittered in the lamplight, dozens of thick coins. Again, Fargo shook his head.

"Sorry about your daughter, or ward, or whatever," Fargo said slowly. "I'm sure you can find somebody else to help you." The count's eyes went dull, and he gathered the gold back into the purse.

"I see I have misjudged you," he said. He bowed stiffly and walked away. When he had gone, Sixty chuckled.

"Don't like Russians?"

"Just a feeling," Fargo said. "About that one."

The fat bartender came by with a loaded tray and put two beers down on the table. Fargo paid up with the gambler's money, and as the bartender started to leave, he pulled up short and turned back, putting the tray down. He patted his vest pocket and extracted an envelope.

"Oh, Mr. Fargo," he said. "I meant to give you this when you came in tonight. It arrived on the afternoon mail run."

Fargo took the envelope. It was tattered and had been pasted over with many stamps. His name was printed in big awkward capital letters. He opened it and read:

> You sed cal if I ever neded help. I do. Com to Alakanuk. Theyrs meny men might dye.
>
>> Yr old frind, MacKenzie.

Fargo read the words several times and then looked at the date of the message—two months before. He swore under his breath.

"Trouble?" Sixty asked.

"Sounds like it," Fargo said. "Up north around the Yukon, your old stomping ground. Old friend, name of Pete MacKenzie."

"MacKenzie!" Sixty squawked. "The hell you say! Pete's in trouble?"

"You know him?"

"Put his first moss diaper on him," Sixty said proudly. "Taught that boy to read the snow myself. Watched him kill his first bear. Haven't seen little Petie-Boy in years." Fargo smiled at the nickname, remembering the huge dark hulk of Pete MacKenzie. "What kind of trouble is it?"

"He doesn't say." Fargo handed him the piece of paper, and Sixty bent over it for several minutes, patiently sounding out the letters. Then he nodded and sat back. They looked at each other.

"I guess I'm going up to the Yukon after all," Fargo said.

"I'm with you," the old man said. "If you're a willing."

Fargo lifted his glass in answer.

"Here's to Petie," Sixty said solemnly.

They clanked the beer mugs together, drank up, and left the bar together.

A week later, Fargo stood on the deck of a schooner and gazed at the dense gray fog. From time to time it cleared, and he could glimpse the towering cliffs and distant mountains of Russian America. Here and there massive glaciers, frozen rivers of ice, wound between the peaks and came down to the water.

"The captain informs me we'll be arriving at Alakanuk in a few minutes," a voice said. Fargo glanced at Count Victoroff who had walked up from behind him. Fargo nodded wordlessly and looked out at the leaden water again as the count moved away.

For a week they'd been on the ship as it made its way up the northwest coast. Several times the count had tried to persuade Fargo to take on the trailblazing job. But Fargo had simply answered that he had other business to take care of and finally Victoroff had given up.

A break between the drifting banks of clouds showed a wide inlet—the mouth of the mighty Yukon. With a creak the boat turned. The white sails snapped in the steady wind and soon the fog lifted. As they sailed into the inlet, Fargo spotted a tiny collection of dwellings on the snow-dappled barren bank. That was the village of Alakanuk. All hands were on deck to lower the sails, and within minutes the ship was easing in toward the dock. Sixty appeared from below hauling their bags of gear, and they disembarked.

There was no hotel in Alakanuk, but Fargo spotted a sign that read ROOMS TO RENT, and Sixty stayed to arrange accommodations while Fargo scouted out the town and asked around for MacKenzie. As he wandered through the tiny village, Fargo spotted fur-jacketed Russian trappers hurrying along in the biting wind, but few Indians. Most were probably out fishing. Ever since the Russians had sailed into the straits two hundred years before, the trappers, the *promyshlenniki,* had ravaged the Indian tribes—the Inuit on the coast and the Ingalik, Tanana, and Koyukon tribes of the interior, sometimes holding hostages in exchange for furs. An uneasy peace had finally come, and in the village of Alakanuk the Indians and Russians huddled side by side on the barren coast, eking out an existence by trading and whaling.

Alakanuk wasn't much to see—a few lumber buildings, a general store that also housed the town bar and post office, a row of sod houses, and the low sod mounds that were the roofs of Inuit dwellings half-buried in the earth. He knew the round houses were constructed of whalebone and driftwood sunk into the ground beneath the domes of thick sod. The Inuit kayaks, called *baidarkas,* lined the rocky beach. At one end of the village stood a Russian church, the onion-shaped dome as gray as the sky.

At the other end was a sprawling camp of more than two dozen dirty canvas tents pitched in the snow and mud. Fargo walked down a passage between the tents and looked about. Dozens of men were loafing around by the campfires, playing cards or whittling. Several were cleaning rifles. They were a tough-looking bunch, hard-eyed, many with scarred faces and missing fingers where the hard living of the north had left its mark on them. Suddenly, he saw a familiar figure approaching, picking his way through the mud and talking to a heavyset bald man. Count Victoroff paused when he spotted Fargo and hurried forward. He wore a full-length beaver coat and thick fur hat, Russian style.

"Mr. Fargo! This is my army," the count said grandly, gesturing around him. "And you see we are well supplied." He swept a hand toward the spot where dozens of sled dogs were staked and piles of provisions awaited loading onto a row of dog sleds. "This is Skye Fargo, the one I was telling you about," the count said to the bald man beside him. The man looked at Fargo with narrowed eyes and then extended his hand, which was hard and callused.

"I'm Buck Slade," he said. "Head of this outfit." Fargo nodded. "Heard you're a good trailblazer. We could use a good tracker." Fargo shrugged and the count cut in.

"Mr. Fargo knows my offer still stands," the count said.

"Yeah," Fargo responded. "Good luck to you." He moved away from them before the count could press him again. At the edge of the camp, he spotted two men leaning against a pile of broken rock. He hailed them.

"Been up here in Alakanuk long?" he asked.

One of them grunted and looked suspiciously at him.

The other said, "Long enough." He tucked some tobacco into his cheek.

"You ever run into a fellow named MacKenzie?" At his name both men jumped a little. "I'm looking for him."

"Why?" one of them asked, his eyes cold.

"Met him a long time ago," Fargo said. The two men looked at each other.

"Yeah, we know Pete. MacKenzie was supposed to be leading this outfit," one of them said. He chewed his plug a long moment. "But now he ain't."

"How come?" Fargo asked, his thoughts whirling. So Pete MacKenzie had been mixed up in the count's rescue mission.

"Ain't you heard? Pete MacKenzie got himself killed," the man said. He turned and spat a yellow stream of tobacco into a snowbank. "Last week."

Fargo glanced across the gray water of the bay for a long moment. Pete MacKenzie dead? "What the hell happened?" Fargo asked.

"Enemies, I guess. Or a woman," one said with a

shrug. He spat again. "That's what they say. But who knows?"

"He'd just come back from a solo trip upriver," the other said. "Trying to find this Russian big shot's daughter. I heard he figured out where she's hid, pretty much. Then he got killed. Now they're looking around for another tracker."

"How'd he die?"

"Go see for yourself," one said. "You'll find him five miles west of here. By the bend of the creek," one said. "What's left of him."

After another moment of silence, Fargo walked away. Snow blew in and was beginning to fall, obscuring the hills to the west. He walked into the general store, picked out some sturdy snowshoes, strapped them on, and started up the creek. He had gone several miles before he thought of Sixty, but it was too late to turn back and fetch him. Instead, Fargo tramped on through the falling snow, to find whatever was left of Pete MacKenzie. And afterward, he'd call on Count Victoroff and find out what the hell was really going on.

"And he found them!" the count said excitedly. "MacKenzie found their secret camp way up the Yukon in the back country, past the Nulato trading post, hidden in the hills."

"So, then you know where they are. Why do you need a tracker?" Fargo asked. Sixty shifted beside him. They were sitting at one of the wooden tables at one side of the general store, which was what passed for a bar in Alakanuk. The gray morning light filtered into the small dirty window.

The count reached into his pocket and pulled out a piece of folded buckskin. He spread it onto the table, and Fargo could see that the skin had been marked with berry dye.

"Some kind of map," Sixty said quietly.

Fargo made out the familiar shape of the Yukon River, snaking inland, and an *X* at about the spot he knew the Ingalik Indian village of Anvik lay. Farther up was a larger *X* where the trading post was and then a series of small dots and pictographs of mountains as the trail left the river and turned due north. Then the markings blurred, the leather stiff where it had been water-soaked.

"You see, the map was damaged, and I can't tell exactly where the camp lies," Victoroff said, tracing the trail with his long finger. "My men could wander around in that wilderness for months and still miss them by a few miles. And the snows are coming in. In another month that country will be impassable."

"Why don't you wait until spring?" Sixty asked.

"I can't leave my daughter with those men for another year," the count said, his eyes blazing. "I can't wait another year for my revenge. *Nyet*. I need somebody to track them now. I need somebody to go up-river with my men and find that camp. Besides, they won't be expecting an attack this time of year. By spring, they might have moved on."

"So," Fargo said quietly, leaning back in his chair. "Who do you think killed Pete MacKenzie?"

The count looked toward the window where the snow was starting to fall against the gray sky.

"Isn't it obvious?" he said, anger seething under his words. "Those thugs. Those criminals who are holding Natasha discovered Pete knew where they were hiding. Maybe they have friends here in Alakanuk. Or maybe they followed him down the Yukon. In any case, he got back alive, and then a day later, he disappeared. They are dangerous men. Evil men." The count's brows lowered, and he looked again at Fargo. "I will hunt them down if it's the last thing I do."

Fargo thought of MacKenzie's frozen corpse hanging from the spruce. And the words of MacKenzie's last message came back to him. That must have been what his message meant—he needed Fargo to come and help with the assault on the Russian gang's hideout. Otherwise, many men, the count's men, would die.

"I'll help you," Fargo said.

The count smiled broadly, pulled out the poke of gold coins, and threw them down on the table.

"Pete MacKenzie was an old friend of mine," Sixty said heartily. "So, I'm coming, too." Fargo noticed that the smile on the count's face flickered for a moment.

"You . . . *knew* Mr. MacKenzie?" Victoroff asked, a slight strain in his voice.

"Why sure," Sixty said. "Everybody in the Yukon knew Pete MacKenzie." Victoroff's face relaxed.

"Da, Da," he said with a laugh.

Fargo felt the slight uneasiness prick him again, the vague idea that everything was not right about this whole deal. And he decided not to tell the count about MacKenzie's message to him. For a moment, he reconsidered taking the job. But now he'd said he'd go. And, damn it, he had to find MacKenzie's killer. Taking the job that MacKenzie was supposed to have done might be the only way to figure out who'd killed him.

Fargo and Sixty rose and left the general store. Outside, a blast of bitter wind swirled the snow around them. Fog was moving in toward shore. Sixty raised his head and sniffed the wind.

"Only October and the snow's coming hard on the coast already," he said, shaking his head. "It's going to be a bad winter. Real bad."

As he followed Sixty toward the camp of the count's men, Fargo glanced toward the hills, partly obscured by the driving snow. Up the Yukon was the most dangerous territory in the world, cold, heartless, and hungry. It would freeze the life out of a man if it could, and every minute out there was a struggle for survival. It would take everything he knew just to get by and a helluva lot of luck to find out what he wanted to know. A hard blast of wind roared around them, and Sixty pulled up short a moment and squinted as his eyes, too, searched inland for the hills obliterated by the blowing snow.

"In winter that territory's meaner than a starving wolf with his teeth sunk in your leg," Sixty muttered under his breath as if reading Fargo's thoughts. They turned toward the camp.